Also by Joe Prosit

Machines Monsters and Maniacs Volume 1

Bad Brains

99 Town, Book One of the "From Order" Series

7 Androids, Book Two of the "From Order" Series

Zero City, Book Three of the "From Order" Series

Look What You Made Me Do

And coming soon…

They Come From Below

MACHINES
MONSTERS
AND
MANIACS
VOLUME II

20 SHORT STORIES

JOE PROSIT

Author Photo by Cadence Porisch, on Instagram @cadey_photography
Contact the author at www.JoeProsit.com or by email at joeprosit@gmail.com.
1st Edition. ISBN 9798334112421

Contents

The Quest Giver

First released on November 1st, 2019, on MedusPod Podcast, Episode 11

"It's dangerous to go alone. Take this."

The kid, and he was just a kid, too young to be called a man, looked funny at the long steel blade resting in my open palms. "What is it?"

Not a head for smarts, this one. He had an unblemished face and youthful beauty. All his days spent maturing and none aging. Oh yes, he was going to need the weapon where he was going. "The last blade handcrafted by the master swordsmith, Masamune, at his forge high atop the Mountains of Mist. Careful. It's honed to a razor's edge, in case the monsters have thick hides."

"Thick hides? Listen mister, I'm not hacking at anybody with no sword."

So petulant. So certain of his purpose in this world, or rather, lack thereof. Apparently, I needed to speak more slowly. "You clearly don't have a handle on the situation in which you find yourself. I said, it's dangerous to go alone."

"Nah. No thanks, man. I think *you're* dangerous," he said while stepping away. When he had backed far enough to bump into the glass door of the pawn shop, he smirked. "Later, weirdo." Then he pushed the door open, slipped out, and was gone.

"Yes. I'll be seeing you again shortly."

6

When the boy left, the pawn shop fell quiet once again. Ambient music plinked and twanged from invisible speakers, only audible when everything else was not. I sighed and slipped the sword back under the counter. He'd be back. They came here to hock car stereos or buy used guitars that would make them stars in their dreams, but in reality, would sit unpracticed in the corners of their rooms. They came in with petty desires and unmotivated dreams but left with so much more.

I have to admit, when the phone rang, it startled me if only for a moment. Only after I answered did I realize how boring the conversation would be.

"Meryl, how good to hear from you," I said after recognizing his voice. He drolled on with his usual complaints and threats, never changing his tune, this one. "Of course, you're always welcome in my humble place of business. Come down anytime."

His voice continued even as I pulled the receiver away from my ear and didn't stop until I set it back in its cradle. Meryl believed nothing in life was more important than his rules and regulations. My time was best spent on other things. And speaking of...

The front door's electric chime binged and bonged, and another character entered the pawn shop. This one was a girl. Big hair. Vapid smile. Short skirt. A suit coat with big shoulder pads. She strolled to the center of the pawn shop like it was a model's runway. She stopped in the middle of all the used electronics and old romance novels, tossed her hair, and winked at me. I nodded back.

She showed no reaction. A few seconds later, she tossed her hair again, flipping it with the back of her fingers, and followed it with another wink.

Ahh. A non-player character. Clichéd, but on cue.

And just as timely, another unwitting hero appeared through the front door. This one also a girl, but not so designed and polished. This one more soaked in her own

7

idiosyncrasies. Hair undone. Shoes untied. Eyes she kept to herself and cast downward whenever not stealing glances sideways. She wore enough black to be a villain, but I knew better. She moved to a selection of old DSL cameras and lenses. The non-player character did her best to show this new girl how well she could flip her hair and wink. The girl by the cameras didn't notice.

But when the three oversized brutes shoved through the door, their crunching footsteps drowning out the bing-bong bell, the girl by the cameras looked up. Perhaps she had potential after all. The three brutes ignored her and moved to the winker and hair flipper. One quick uppercut to the gut and she crumpled over. The middle brute caught her before she had a chance to fall to the linoleum. He slung her over his wide muscular shoulder like a sack of potatoes. And once they had her, the three about-faced and strutted back out the door having not said a word.

The girl by the cameras, her eyes, wide and alert now, stabbed out from under her overhanging bangs. Her back was pressed against the shelves. "Jesus Christ!" she said as soon as the non-player characters were gone.

"Quick! They've taken the mayor's daughter!" I said to her.

"What the—?" the girl said to me. "Aren't you going to call the cops?"

"After them! They have the mayor's daughter!" I said, emoting as much as I could.

"Forget that, old man. I'm calling the cops and getting the hell outta here," she said, dug out a cell phone, and fled to the exit. I watched her go out of the door and check up and down the sidewalk. She took a step in the opposite direction of the brutes and the kidnapped girl. Then doubled back and broke into a sprint after them.

The boy who would go alone to dangerous places nearly knocked into her as he came charging back into the pawn shop. His face was pale. His eyes electric.

8

"How much?" he hurried me. "How much for the sword?"

As if the weapon had never left my hands, I raised my open palms above the counter and displayed Masamune's last work of art to the boy. "It's dangerous to go alone. Take this."

"Yeah, you said it! How much?"

"No charge. But do not dawdle. Adventure awaits," I told him, and this time he listened.

The boy snatched the blade and held it aloft for just one frozen moment. In the measure of stilled time, the steel emitted an unearthly gleam and sang like a tight violin string. When the moment had passed, he looked only slightly more bewildered than he'd been when he first returned to the shop. But he didn't let the second of sentience-betrayal distract him. He brought the hilt of the weapon down to his solar plexus.

"Thanks, old man," the boy said and rushed out the door.

Another satisfied customer.

He was barely out the door when Meryl entered. Meryl. That bureaucrat. Tall, plain-faced, dull hair, a somehow boring and featureless black trench coat, and dark sunglasses: an appearance that was almost a non-appearance, a man you only thought you saw. He approached the counter with a confidence and a smirk that crawled under my skin.

"Hello, Meryl," I said.

Behind him, the door bing-bonged, and another unknowing adventurer came closer to his destiny. A teenage boy. Not from the city. Flannel and jeans. Long uncombed hair.

"Hello, Adalrich," Meryl said. "Up to your old tricks again, I see."

"Tricks? What tricks?" I asked.

9

Behind Meryl, a TV popped to life in front of the be-flanneled youth. His eyes locked on the screen. In an instant, he forgot whatever trivialities had occupied his life before this fateful moment. The entire width of the forty-two-inch monitor was consumed by the image of Sky Admiral Angus CloudCleaver. "Red Alert! Red Alert! The evil Xikicrons have invaded the Galactic Colonies. All pilots to their starfighters! This means *you!*" Just outside the pawnshop, a beam of light came down and shone on a plastic quarter-operated amusement ride molded in the shape of a rocket ship.

"What tricks?" Meryl turned from the boy and his starfighter to me. "Come on, Adalrich. Do we really have to play this game?"

My eyes were still on the boy, whose eyes were flashing between the ride, the TV, and the two of us at the counter. The TV was looping its message over and over again now, short blasts of static between each of the Sky Admiral's alerts. When I caught the boy's eyes, I chinned in the direction of the amusement ride, encouraging him on. They all needed an extra push from time to time.

"Adalrich," Meryl snapped at me.

"Meryl, we both know I'm too old to change my ways. I've been around this globe for too long. I'm not like these brave-hearted souls who come to me. They're just beginning their journeys that will shape and develop them. Me? I've had my arc. I've fixed my beliefs."

"Stop," Meryl said. "You've been warned, reprimanded, fined, and sanctioned. The next step is to shut you down and bring you in. Is that what you want?"

Blatherings. I heard it all before and none of it interested me. My eyes were still on the boy. I waited for his decision. When I saw his confusion beat out his curiosity and drive his feet through the door and away from the quarter-operated amusement ride, my shoulders slouched.

I sighed. "Why are you here, Meryl?"

"Haven't you been listening to a word I've said? I'm here to shut you down, Adalrich. I promised the counsel I'd come here and find you abiding by the terms of your probation. That you'd learned your lesson. That you'd only issue out adventure by the approved means. Books. Movies. Stories planted inside their minds by hypnotic suggestions. You know, how the rest of us do it. But here you are, quest-giving again like a bearded old wizard."

"They need it," was all I said. All I felt I needed to say.

"It's dangerous, Adalrich. There's a boy out there swinging a katana at ravenous monsters in the street. Right outside your store."

I leaned an ear towards the front of the shop. Of course, there were the quiet ambient sounds of guitars, sitars, and shamisens playing peacefully in the store. But now that he mentioned it, I did hear the distant sounds of screams, the growling of beasts, the clanging of steel, and the whine of police sirens in the distance. I shrugged. "Someone had to kill those monsters."

"Adalrich, there *were* no monsters until you issued them out. Just like there were no kidnapped mayor's daughters and no invading Xikicrons until you created them. You're causing all this, and a lot of people are noticing," Meryl said.

"Sometimes I create evil for them to defeat. Sometimes I send them against pre-existing evils. So what?" I shrugged.

"So what? So last time I brought you in, you signed an affidavit specifically stating you'd stop creating real-life dangers for susceptible frail humans like these wanderers and vagabonds who come strolling through your door. Fiction! Adalrich. You signed the affidavit swearing you were going to stick with fiction. And now I come here and see this nonsense. And there's no way I can hide this. No way I can cover it up or brush it under the rug. You…" He stopped. "What?"

I held up a finger. Long, thin of flesh but thick of knuckle.

"What is that supposed to mean?" Meryl asked.

"It means nothing, but I have to correct you. The term you're looking for is 'heroes.'"

"Heroes?" Meryl repeated. "When did I ever say anything about—"

"Susceptible, frail humans. Wanders. Vagabonds. That's what you called them," I said. "But the term you were looking for is 'heroes.'"

Behind Meryl's back, the young man in the flannel crept back into view, just outside the glass storefront. He on the left. The quarter-operated starfighter on the right. Ever so slowly, he stepped closer to the fighter.

"And what happens when one of your heroes gets killed?" Meryl said.

I didn't mean to roll my eyes. It was just that he was so tiresome. "I give them extra lives, Meryl."

Frustrated, he tried another attack from another front. "They didn't ask for you to interfere in the life they had! They come in this shop to look for a cheap deal. To make a few quick bucks. To waste time. To sift through the debris of other safe terrestrial lives. Not to be sent on some wild goose chase by a crazed old man."

"And you approve of that sort of life?" I took my eyes off the youth outside and fixed them on Meryl. "Of common lives lived commonly? Of time wasted looking for cheap deals or swapping stolen goods for worthless paper money? If that's what you'd like for yourself, I have all the paper money you can carry," I popped open the register and began shoveling dollars and euros and pesos and dinars and yen out onto the counter.

"Here. Take it. If this is what our lives amount to, I should consider mine fulfilled, and you should consider yourself lucky to have come in today."

"Put that— Adalrich! Quit it. Put this money—" Meryl shoved at the bills mounding on the counter. I kept shoveling. Some of it spilled over to the floor. Some of it he managed to grab and throw back at me. "Stop this insanity right now!"

I slammed my fist through the money and against the display case. Before my fist met glass, every scrap of money vanished from floor to counter to register. Uncushioned by currency, the glass cracked. My eyes locked on Meryl's. "This world has been without true adventures for too long and you know it. It is decaying their souls. They lumber about without mission or purpose. Without pride or perspective. They are gorged with money and wealth and peace and pacified by poor electronic simulations, but they have never tasted the one food that will truly make them whole, the meal that will feed their spirits and banish the likes of you back from whence you came. They've never tasted true adventure."

"And they never will. Not while I'm here," Meryl said. "There's a cost to the product you sell, and it's got nothing to do with money. Pain. Misery. Destruction. Loss of life. You con them out of their norm like the crooked pawnbroker you pretend to be. You think you're so noble but look around! You think it's all a façade, but this is exactly who you are. An old man hocking broken goods to broken people."

"So leave me be," I said. "I enjoy being this old man, hocking these old ideas of danger and far-off destinations. If I'm an obsolete relic of a time long forgotten, then forget me. Leave me to the waste bin of legend."

"And what about this?" Meryl half turned and stretched a palm out to the youth and the starfighter. The boy climbed inside, and as he did, the craft grew around him. A poly-carbon alloy airframe unsheathed around the plastic molding of the child's ride. A

13

canopy highlighted with laser-green electronic readouts slid over his head and sealed him inside. He strapped into a flight harness and began flicking switches like he was born to fight the Xikicrons. Thrusters fired and rumbled to life against the sidewalk. Launch in t-minus five... "What am I supposed to do about that?" Meryl asked.

"Nothing," I said. Four. "We're clear of the blast-off area." Three. "But I would advert your eyes." Two. "The ion thrusters are rather bright."

One. White smoke consumed the starfighter a moment before it punched spaceward and out of the atmosphere in one supernova-bright flash. We were left deafened by the roar and blinded by the blaze. The exhaust cloud choked the entire street and blocked any view beyond the shop windows.

"That's it, Adalrich. That's the last straw," Meryl pointed a finger at me. "We've known each other a long time, and I've given you more than ample opportunity to change your ways. But you've worn out my patience. I'm taking you in."

The cloud outside the shop was slow to dissipate. It hung there like a thick fog, and through it, four short humanoid shapes began to take form.

"Okay. I'll go quietly," I said to Meryl and stuck out both wrists, ready to be cuffed. "But before we go, answer me this. Do you really think I'm the only one who still has a taste for pitfalls and perilous journeys? For heroism? For adventure? Do you really think I'm the last quest giver?"

"Don't be so proud of yourself. Your kind are a dime a dozen," Meryl said and went about fishing handcuffs out of a back pocket. He slapped one cuff onto a wrist.

"And who do you think us quest givers send our adventurers out to protect?" I asked him. "Don't you think we have each other's backs? Who, Meryl, down here on this terrestrial plain, has your back?"

14

The pawn shop door binged and bonged. Meryl turned. The cloud had thinned enough to show us four young human silhouettes and the familiar outline of BMX bikes leaned up against the windows. As the first boy entered, smoke from the ion thrusters rolled in with him and his crew. Another boy followed, he with a flashlight and a bandana tied around his head. The third member was a girl with a ponytail and a slingshot at arm's length. The fourth held an accident time-yellowed map.

"You sure this is the right place?" the first boy said.

"I'm sure of it! The map leads right here," the last answered, his eyes never leaving the sand-colored sheet of parchment.

"To the lair of the Man in Black," flashlight boy said.

Slingshot girl stepped around him and pulled the rubber bands of her weapon taunt. "We've come a long ways for you, Meryl. We're here to send you back from whence you came."

"Don't you see, Meryl?" I smiled at him. "I just send out the call to adventure. They're the ones who answer."

Permanence

First published in March 2024 in Corner Bar Magazine

It's a matter of permanence. Always has been. And it's what I've never been. Got started with in-town deliveries. Drove long haul for years. Switched to taxi when a lady friend moved to the big city. Hated it. Went back to in-town deliveries. Hate that. Hated her for it. Dropped her. Went back to long haul.

Got a new lady. A new place out in the sticks. Had some kids. She left. Kids left. But to be fair, I left twice a week for the road. A distribution center in Des Moines. A warehouse in Omaha. A plant in Gary. A shipping harbor in Duluth. Department stores in Billings, Manitowoc, Ann Arbor, Sioux City, Sparta, Eau Claire, Columbus, New Ulm, North Platte, Marquette... Places with Indian names, French names, German names. Places named after other places and other cities and other people that didn't exist anymore. Here. There. Everywhere. But I always meant to come home. It was just, one of those times, home left before I could get back.

Some dogs are just meant to roam, I guess.

Through my windshield, I watch the consistency of others. Same buildings. Same houses. Same yards. Same kids' toys scattered in the green grass or the dried leaves or under the mounds of snow.

Somewhere east of Aberdeen, there's a house with metal sculptures in the front yard. Home of not just an artist, but a welder. Maybe even a historian, or save that, an archivist. Most of the things there, built from polished steel or chrome, are nameless things that represent nothing more than the shape of the metal and the state of the maker's mind. Some twist and corkscrewing and dance like a tornado or maybe a stripper on a pole. Others are rigid landmarks, obelisks and monoliths as motionless as Stonehenge, which only mark the motion of other, much larger things. Maybe they even mark my motion as I drive on by.

Over the years, her collection has grown. It started out simple. An ordinary windmill. An ornate weathervane. A sculpture of a dog. Maybe a memorial to a beloved and passed-on pet. How was I to know? I never stopped. Never even saw the artist at work. On a trip west, there was a blank space in the grass. On the return trip east, a piece of art full of rotations and revolution that could have been a model of a faraway unfamiliar solar system, all of it glistening under our own familiar sun, danced where the blank space had been.

That collection was a metallic garden, growing before my eyes in the slowest stop-motion animation ever recorded.

The job doesn't change. Not really. Cities change. Some grow. Some die. Thunder Bay. Lincoln. Wichita. Lafayette. Bismarck. Baudette. South Bend. Kalamazoo. People around them change. Those I've met. Those I've gotten to know. Those I learned to love. Those I grew to hate. All gone eventually and replaced by new people who I might love or hate someday in the future.

The things I haul change, but those things have never concerned me. The thing that hauls me changes too, and that concerns me more. Driving in-town deliveries, it was always a box truck. Of course, when I drove taxi, it was a taxi. When I went long haul, it was always a bobtail, naturally, but behind it was sometimes a flatbed, sometimes a reefer trailer, sometimes a low boy, sometimes just a regular old dry van. They kept changing the rigs though. Flat-nosed were big for a while through the 80's, then they went back to long-nosed, and I gotta say, I always had a soft spot for the ones with the bulldog hood ornament. Like it was standing guard, on the lookout for anything in my way that might cause trouble.

What was next was rigs with no driver at all. Of course, I wasn't in 'em, but I saw 'em. Fewer and fewer of my kind on the road. Fewer and fewer truck stops, diners, and skeezy gentlemen's clubs that never had any gentlemen in 'em to begin with. More and more of just rigs and loads. More and more money for the bosses. Fewer jobs for the diehards like me. Everything moves. Everything changes. Everything but me. But things only really changed when I stopped moving.

Truck broke down east of Aberdeen. Blown a gasket and sat steaming on the shoulder of the highway, and wouldn't you know it, there was that metal garden of ever-moving sculptures just one ditch away. Ever since the robot trucks took over the majority of the workload, companies don't provide much support for old dogs like us. So there I sat, motionless and helpless. Until the sculptor came out.

A woman, who woulda guessed? Not I said the fly. We chatted. What about doesn't much matter. Conversations, they have all the permanence of an oakleaf in October. But she was nice. Brought me in. Fed an old man a sandwich. Showed me her workshop. Showed me a forge where even the most stubborn metals get soft and flexible and fluid. Where even steel can move. Then, I don't know why, but I'm not ungrateful, she pushed me in.

And finally, I changed. From wrinkled skin, rotten teeth, and fragile bones to something fluid and pliable, and also something rigid and strong. I was a thing made not to move, set in motion by dozens of hinges and joints and pivots and springs. I grew up from a blank spot of grass, a new addition to a garden that will never wilt. I revolve and rotate and oscillate and gyrate like a stripper or a tornado or a whole solar system. I gleam under our familiar but restless sun. I mark days and months and years and eons and epochs, never moving but never motionless.

An old dog learnt new tricks. Permanence.

The Dream Theater

First published in December 2023 in Möbius Blvd

The problem with live theater was that it was a collaborative art. A show wasn't a show without actors, directors, set designers, grips, lighting and sound technicians, costumes, hair and make-up, prop master, choreographer, music director, the band… Every one of them had a job to do, and every one of them had to do that job perfectly to pull off a perfect show. And they were all so eager to screw it up.

Sam was amongst those people but not of those people. He wasn't "The Director," the guy in the canvas and pine chair giving actors feedback on their performances, adjusting the script, tweaking the score so it fit his vision of the show, and bowing at center stage after all the roses had been thrown and the whole cast all but begged him to his spotlight and whose name was high and center on the playbill. That wasn't Sam. Sam was the stage director. The one responsible for ushering actors to the left or the right wing and cueing their entrances and exits. The one synchronizing the music and the lighting mid-performance. The one ensuring the costume changes happened in the right order at the right times, and that they happened on time, and when they didn't happen on time, telling the performers who were still on stage to stretch out the scene, to milk their lines, to stall, to give the lead performer struggling with the giant ball gown time to fight with the zipper and find the right wing. And he was the one who made the call when the ball gown ripped and the correct wig was "Gone! Just gone!" to either send the lead out with a taped-up dress and without a wig, or to drop the curtains for an unscheduled intermission.

The actors, the band, the lights, the set dressers… they each had their own little part to play. And Sam's job? His job was to play all of them.

"A theater for your dreams," the man said. Although, he didn't look like a man much acquainted with any theater. His exterior was rotund and guff. He clipped his words so instead of saying, "theater" it came out more like "tea-ate-her."

He sold wood carvings, presumably but not necessarily of his own making. All across the table were small sculptures of endless subjects: turtles with detailed shells, dolphins jumping over waves, fairies fluttering on flower petals, big-bellied Buddhas, Christs on crucifixes with crowns of thorns, puzzle boxes with hidden pieces that slid to allow the next piece to rotate and reveal a button that would eventually open the lid. They were all very intricate and well-crafted in that dark-stained wood. None of them interested Sam. He had no need for such things. He only came here because sometimes young upstart artists sold rare and brilliant prints for cheap. When the sculpture salesman called him out from the crowd and lured him over by the means of the time-tested sales technique known as "the hard sell," Sam was more than dubious. He was utterly confident that this particular hawker wasn't going to separate this particular fool from his money.

After all, wasn't this all a little too on-the-nose? Even the name "bazaar" was a bit much. It was a farmer's market. A sidewalk sale. A flea market. An exaggerated garage sale. Oh, Sam got the schtick. Use a word like "bazaar" and people expected

21

things to be, well, bizarre. Sprinkle in a little old-world colonialism, a dash of unconscious racism, and a vaguely foreign and exotic word like "bazaar" and now you've excited people's imagination. At a farmer's market, you might buy fresh vegetables, locally sourced honey, or hand-made crafts. At a flea market, you'll find old electronics, passed-down jewelry, and vintage clothes. But at a bazaar? Bazaars were where you looked for magic lamps, religious relics, enchanted artifacts, and cursed taxidermy from strange, distant, faraway lands! Why, the seller of the carvings should have had a dangling, white, fu-man-chu mustache, a long-stemmed pipe, and incense burning inside ornate brass pots hanging from chains around his shop. He should have warned him about the dangers of his purchase in whispers between shifting glances.

It wasn't anything like that, of course. The salesman was pedestrian, boring, and wore a t-shirt with the name of his website screen printed on the chest. He had a pot belly and a five o'clock shadow. His eyes were yellowed and a bit dim. The bulbous mole on his neck had sprouted three wiry hairs. He didn't even have an over-the-top, offensive accent. More interstate trucker than Silk Road spice merchant. Still, there were hints of all those more stereotypical trappings of bazaars. Someone was cooking with too much curry. Incense and oils burned from the booth next door. A few folks were speaking Mandarin. Others Spanish. Others were shopping for imitation Afghan rugs. Like how a community theater might come close to pulling off a Broadway performance, it only required a bit of suspense of disbelief, and you were there, seeing the genuine article, alongside Ali Baba and the Forty Thieves in a Baghdad marketplace.

"Sumthin' just for you," the man said and spun on his stool away from Sam.

Sam saw nothing that spoke to him in the least. What would he even do with a wooden carving of a human skull that opened as if ready for a full lobotomy? Was it an ashtray? A place to put your car keys? Who would buy such a thing? Then, the salesman swiveled back to face Sam, and he had an item he held close to his navel.

"What is that?" Sam asked.

"What's it look like? It's a stage," the man said. "A whole theater, actually. See?"

The man held the carving a little closer to Sam, and a little further from his navel, as if the thing were a newborn baby that needed its neck supported and could not be fumbled.

Sam did see. The piece of wood wasn't large, maybe the size of half a loaf of bread, but exquisitely detailed, nevertheless. The curtains looked frozen in billowy motion. There were seams on the stage floor. The apron curved outward toward the audience in a graceful arch. The wings waited in darkness for a stage director with headset and clipboard to send out the next line of dancers or actors. Better than any community theater, this theater all but demanded Sam envision the perfect production taking place on its miniature stage.

"How much?" Sam said, surprised when he found his wallet already opening up in his hand.

If he'd been smart, if he'd been streetwise enough to remember that this was a bazaar and the next scene in its screenplay was labeled "haggling" he probably could have gotten the sculpture for half of what he paid. The phrase "Jewing him down," came to his mind, and he was immediately disgusted that it had. Sam wasn't interested in "talking down" the salesman and throwing prices back and forth until they agreed on a number the salesman already had in mind before they began. After all, you didn't haggle at a farmer's market or a flea market. Why should a bazaar be any different? No. He paid the full asking price and felt better for it.

When that was all said and done and the sculpture was wrapped in a plastic grocery sack and tucked under Sam's arm, the salesman, perhaps hurt by having to skip his favorite part of the play, doubled down on the next scene: The Ominous Warning.

"I hope you like it, pal. That isn't just any theater," he said.

"Is it modeled after any real-world stage? The proportions–"

And before the salesman spoke again, the haze washed away from his eyes. Like he'd opened a second reptilian inner eyelid, the fog clear and his pupil focused in crisp contrast to the whites. "Only the one in your mind. The one that performs the script you write each night while you sleep and goes onstage each morning when you wake up," he said.

"Huh," Sam said. "Because the proportions are almost identical to the place where I–"

"Enjoy your purchase, pal," the man said, his eyes suddenly dim and dull again. "I got other items for other customers I gotta get to."

And then Sam was fading back into the crowd, and the salesman was hard selling to others, calling them out by the color of their shirt or by a hat that they wore, reeling in anyone who looked his way as if curiosity was as physical a thing as a fishing line and a lure.

Once he was back in his apartment, Sam placed the sculpture on the shelf above his desk. It made a good bookend if nothing else, and perhaps when work became too frustrating, he could take it down and imagine how a botched show could have gone better.

He didn't think about dreams until early the next morning, before sunrise, before he got up to make coffee, while his subconscious was still stage-directing his imagination. It wasn't a particularly creative script, as far as dreams go. Pretty standard fare, really. The subconscious's old time-tested tale of being naked at work. Oh, he still had his clipboard and headset, and an all-black pair of tennis shoes, but between his laces and his lips? Nothing but a clipboard and a birthday suit. And of course, he couldn't stop in his tasks to put something on. No, he had to go about shuffling performers from one side of backstage to the other, this one from the right wing to the left, this one over to costume, this one out of the way to allow for the dance line to come on stage. All the while his own star of the show swung between his legs while the cast and crew threw him confused and repulsed glares. Worst of them all came from Marie, the young understudy who looked so betrayed and hurt by his sudden nudity. He wanted to explain to them that this just happened, that he couldn't change it, that they should ignore his nudity and focus on their jobs, or they were going to miss their cues. Of course, none of them were professional enough for that.

The choreographer even had the audacity to wonder aloud, "Why is it so small?"

And then it was over. Not the performance, but the dream. And thank Christ for that. The only thing more disturbing than imagining himself trying to do his job without a thread of clothing was trying to sort out why his mind produced such a scenario to begin with. So, he did his best to forget it. And as dreams went, most of the details stayed there in bed while he got up and staggered into the kitchen and to the coffee machine. It was a comfort to realize that he was still wearing what he'd gone to bed in: an old T-shirt from a previous production and a loose-fitting pair of basketball shorts.

"So small," he scoffed. His package wasn't small. It was tight. The ignorant said David's package was small, but Michelangelo and anyone capable of any research knew

David's penis and testicles looked the way they did because he was ready for battle, and that's what adrenaline did to a man. David was ready for battle, and so was Sam any time he stepped backstage. "It wasn't small," he repeated to himself. "It was tight."

Only after a few good minutes of staring into the abyss over the steaming rim of his coffee did Sam have the wherewithal to wander over to his desk and office chair. There were a few morning rituals he needed to go through to start his day off on the right foot, emails, calendar examinations, and such. After a few sips of joe, those tasks would be no work at all. He didn't get to the part where he sat down in front of his computer, however. A step away from the desk, he froze in place.

There on his bookshelf just above his monitors was the wooden carving he'd bought from the melodramatic bazaar the day before. That was nothing in and of itself. He'd put it there. Of course, it would be there. Although the wooden stage wasn't something he was used to seeing quite yet, it wasn't the simple chunk of wood that paralyzed him in his place. It was what was on the stage that stiffened him as solid as David.

Tiny ballet dancers, all on even smaller demi-pointe tip toes, made their way onto the stage from the right wing. They were the color of the wood, patterned in the grain of the wood, but moved with the grace and poise of the best of dance troupes. They were elegant. They were synchronized. They were precise. They were beautiful. But they were made of wood. And they weren't alone. A soloist flowed out from the left wing, coming before the line of dancers, and took center stage. By her emotions and gestures, she was singing, belting out a crescendo even, but Sam heard nothing. So strange the wood could flex enough to walk and wave and dance, but not enough to sing.

What was he talking about? All of it was strange! So strange it could only be a hallucination. Or an illusion. Perhaps they were some expertly hidden wind-up toys like the trapeze set of a flea circus. That made more sense than anything else. The fluid motions of the singer and dancers had to be an optical illusion. Their actions only that of pre-wound gears and springs. A carnival trick. Clever, and masterfully crafted, but nothing that came from beyond the realm of rational reality.

Engrossed, he leaned in closer, looking for tracks in the floor of the wooden stage, tiny hinges in the legs and arms of the dancers, or wires guiding the gestures of the soloist. Seeing none, he thought that perhaps they weren't wood at all but only mocked up to be wood. They had to be made of silicon rubber or silk, something flexible but painted the color and grain of the rest of the stage.

All in concert, the performers were too many to examine as a whole. Sam picked out the ballet dancer of the far left and watched for flaws to give up the glamor of it all. And there were flaws. Only, not the mechanical sort he searched for. The far left dancer missed a step, fell flat on her heel when she should have remained up high on her toes, and slipped out of sync for just a moment with all the rest.

Another motion caught his eyes, further from center stage, waiting in the wing.

A minuscule stage director stood there in the recesses, out of view of the audience and only visible to Sam when he looked at the theater from a sharp angle. As he leaned to one side, peering around the curtain, he gained a full view of the stage director as the tiny thing waved to others farther backstage, buried deeper in the wood. And the next thing Sam noticed sent his still-hot cup of coffee crashing to the desk surface.

The stage director was nude.

He had his tiny little clipboard and his sliver of a headset and a pair of practical tennis shoes and a microscopic penis protruding from an unkempt bush of pubic hair, and oh it was indeed very small, and nothing else.

27

"Nope!" Sam said, a declaration more than an objection. A statement denying the reality of what he was seeing. An utter rejection of what was before him.

He abandoned the things playing out on this trinket of a theater on his shelf. He needed to turn his attention to the disaster on his desk anyway. The coffee mug had shattered into porcelain shards, and the coffee was seeping between all the keys on the keyboard and staining papers and bills. Sam was all too willing to leave his home office for a roll of paper towels in his kitchen. To return, he was less eager, but compelled by the dripping of coffee off the desk and down to the hardwood floor. He busied himself by unfurling towels off the roll and yanking them free and cramming them down on his keyboard to hopefully suck some of the fluid out from the cracks. Then he was holding the thing up like a dead animal and watching the coffee drip down to the growing puddling around his feet. Then it was back to pulling more paper towels off the roll and sopping up more coffee before it stained everything on the desk.

Sam only glanced back at the stage once during his mopping up, and he regretted it enough not to look again. The stage director in his shoes and headset, holding his clipboard over his genitals now, was being shoved out to the apron of the stage for all the audience to see. The dancers, soloists, set dressers, and even the interns were pointing at him, laughing, and throwing things his way. And was there some tiny little audience somewhere, all in shock at what was before them, or just Sam who saw this performance?

He would have preferred neither, and so turned away with wads of wet, dripping, paper towels for the kitchen garbage can.

Sam avoided his desk and the wooden stage for the rest of the morning. The few daily tasks he had planned could wait till the next morning, or the morning after that if necessary. On his way out the door to work at the real theater where he was always fully

28

and professionally dressed, his eyes passed over the thing he'd taken from the bazaar. The stage was empty. The wings were vacant. Nothing moved. And that was well enough.

Sam didn't particularly enjoy drinking, but a few cocktails did seem to have one desirable effect on him: deep, uninterrupted, dreamless sleep. Back late in the evening from his time spent at the theater, he kicked off his tennis shoes, turned on some senseless reality TV show, made himself a double pour of a gin and tonic, and sat deep into his couch. His desk with the wooden theater was across the apartment, in line-of-sight, but too small and too dimly lit for him to watch it for little performers. Instead, he sipped his cocktail and tried to keep his mind on more pleasant things.

The reality show only held his attention for so long. Eventually, inevitably, his mind went back to his day at work. The company was working on an off-Broadway musical production, ambitious in its sets, costumes, and musical numbers, which made things fun for Sam. A lot of balls to keep juggling in the air. Rehearsals were going well. The performers were talented and dedicated, so much so that Sam felt like he could take his eyes away from the stage from time to time. And there was that understudy who'd been quite friendly with him. Marie, a beautiful woman somewhat new to the world of live theater, had taken an interest in just how he managed to keep everything straight and everyone on their cues. Her eyes batted. Her smile grew. The alcohol in his drink made the memory of her all the more defined.

And a solution to a nagging problem suddenly came to Sam's mind. Perhaps the booze would send him into a sleep so comatose he'd have no dreams. Or… if he went to bed with his mind focused in the direction of his choosing, what he might find on the little wooden stage the next morning wouldn't be so disturbing. Maybe not disturbing whatsoever. Sam took a long and greedy swallow of the gin and tonic and leaned his head back against the stuffing of the couch.

Right at sunrise, his bedroom door exploded outward, slamming against the wall, and exposing the rest of Sam's apartment to his blurry eyes.

"Jesus Christ, no. Don't be there," he mumbled.

But he had to see. He had to check if the company of the dream theater was once again on stage. Sam rushed over to his desk and crashed into his chair as he leaned in close to the tableau.

Sam had to get close to see. If he'd had any far-sightedness the details would have been lost to his faulty vision. But alas, Sam had never needed reading glasses and the fine features of the characters were all too visible. There they were, the two tiny performers, on center stage, hard at work, performing their roles. There was a lone bed with a metal rail headboard and plain white cotton sheets, well, a *wooden* metal rail headboard and *wooden* cotton sheets. And on top of the bed? There was the stage director again, still wearing just shoes and a headset, now with his clipboard neglected on stage right. And underneath the stage director? The big curly hair. The short body. Even the veins in the arms and legs were recognizable. Underneath the stage director, taking a real pounding, was his mother.

"Oh, Jesus! Why?" Sam shouted to his empty apartment. He whirled away from the lurid scene and, pulling his own hair, continued his self-interrogation. "Why? Why would you dream of something like… something like… something like that! What is wrong with me?"

But it was just a dream. Some wild misguided connections firing inside his latent mind. It wasn't real. It wasn't that he wanted to… to… God, he couldn't even say

30

it. It was supposed to be Marie, the pretty, little, ambitious understudy. Not this abomination of an Oedipus Rex reproduction! Sam was at his kitchen sink by now, and the fractured remains of yesterday's coffee mug still sat in the basin. He grabbed the biggest chunk of it, the chunk with the handle still attached, and wound up like a major league fast baller. He flung the remains of the coffee cup the full distance across the apartment and nailed the strike zone, dead on.

What was left of the mug shattered into smaller fragments. The little wooden stage bounced off the back wall, fell to the desk, and tumbled to the coffee-stained floor. It was still in one piece, but certainly, the impact was enough to send its performers off the stage, off the bed, and most importantly, off of each other. But, oh god, what if there was now a minute version of him and his mother hidden somewhere in the cracks of his wood floor, still humping away like dogs and a dog park? And what if he stepped on them? Well, maybe that would be for the best. Just so long as he never had to look upon that, or dream of that, ever again.

Slowly, cautiously, Sam stalked across his apartment to where the theater lay. His knees popped when he crouched down to pick it up. With eyes clamped shut, he picked it up and turned it over in his hand. He heard nothing, which gave him no peace. The soloist had been silent the morning before, and thank all the deities above and below the Earth, he'd been spared from hearing any grunts and moans and squeaking bedsprings this morning. He opened his eyes.

The stage was empty. The bed and both its occupants were gone. The show was over. All that remained beyond the stiff wooden stage curtains was a deep gouge left by the thrown coffee cup piece. Sam sighed, set the toy stage on his desk, and wandered back to his bedroom. Some things were best placed out of mind. As soon as fucking possible.

When Sam stepped through his apartment door, he brought with him a fresh bottle of dry gin and the continuation of an already half-hour-long phone conversation.

"I just wish we were closer, is all," his mom told him through the bud in his ear.

"Mom, we have a good relationship," he said, really not enjoying where this was going.

"I remember when I used to hold you and you'd sleep next to me all night in my bed," she said.

"Mom–"

"I know, I know. That was a long time ago. But that doesn't me we shouldn't spend more time together," she carried on even as he set the bottle of gin on the counter and stole glances at the theater sitting on his desk.

"We can," he promised but didn't mean it. "We will," he said as if a more firmly stated lie would make it anything but. "I've just been really busy with this upcoming show. Today was hell. Anything that could go wrong, did, and I can't help but feel like–"

"You've always been so talented, Sam. You've always wanted things to be so big and perfect. I've always said even as you were growing up, you're always big enough for me. You make your mother very happy, did you know that?" she said, too close to innuendo for his comfort.

It wasn't as if his mother wanted anything other than innocence, but everything she said was twisted inside his stupid brain. But it was all just in his head. His perverse and depraved head that generated that nightmare. But restricted to the space between his ears. And the dream theater.

He eyed it suspiciously. His mother's voice drained away. The theater sat dead on the desk. No performers stirred inside of it. The gouge from the broken coffee cup was evidence that it could be damaged. Despite its "bazaar" origins, the thing wasn't magic. It was just an empty place where he'd been projecting his unconscious insecurities. That was all. And if it had earthly and terrestrial weaknesses, then he could use earthly and terrestrial means to dispose of it.

"Mom, I gotta go. We'll be together again soon," Sam said and hit the "END" button on the call. Together? Why had he used that word? Couldn't he have said, "I'll see you soon," or "We'll talk later,"? Why did he say they'd be together? That was a weird word choice, wasn't it? The screw-on cap of the gin bounced off the countertop and spun on the floor. The rim of the bottle touched his lips.

The day's rehearsals had gone exceptionally poor. Missed cues. Forgotten lines. Out-of-step dance routines. Bickering backstage. And he was at the center of it all. Pulling set dressers one way, pushing costumers the other, and herding dancers and singers all around backstage. And amongst it, what had he heard? Marie. And what had she asked?

"Why is it so small?"

The question wasn't directed toward him, of course. Why would it be? She was talking to the lead actress for whom she understudied. What it was that was so small, Sam didn't know, but surely it had nothing to do with him. After all, what had his mother told him?

"You're always big enough for me."

Ugh! Why couldn't he get that dream, and the previous dream for that matter, out of his head? He let a breath of air out of his lungs. The air bubbled to the bottom of the upturned bottle as if the gin were an office water cooler. It burned all the way down.

33

But the little theater looked empty now, and he hadn't dreamed or even slept since waking up that morning. Surely, his subconscious hadn't populated it already. He brought the bottle with him across his apartment and almost dropped it when he caught a toe on his floor. It tripped him enough to send him to the floor. The pungent liquor splashed over his shirt and face and burned his eyes.

"What the hell?"

Right there in the middle of his living room was a yard-long gouge as if it had been attacked with a chainsaw. When the hell had that happened? How had it happened? It wasn't there this morning. Now a thick and rough scar ran diagonally across his living room.

"Is someone here?" his words echoed through the vacant space.

Who would be here? Who even knew where he lived? And if someone did know where he lived, why would they sneak in just to destroy his floor? It wasn't a large apartment. The only places he couldn't see from where he sat were the bedroom and the bathroom. He picked himself up and took down another long swallow of gin. On the way to the kitchen, he glanced at the stage on his desk. Empty.

For now.

Waking up hungover had one advantage: Sam couldn't remember his dreams. And doing what the booze had done to him, which felt like getting clobbered over the head with a steel shovel, had the added bonus of relieving his mind of the stress over the little carved stage still sitting on his desk.

His trek from the bedroom to the kitchen was focused, even if it wasn't a straight path. He staggered for the sink where he stuck his head under the tap and gulped at the flowing water like a camel. No finesse or decency or sense of stage presence here.

34

Just a greedy sucking in as much cool, rust-tinged water as he could take, like a kid at a garden hose. With each gasp for air between swallows, his head pounded like a kettle drum. Only after the water failed to ease the pounding, did he pull himself away and shut off the tap. His hands fumbled with the coffee and the coffee maker, and in the clearing fog, fragments of his dreams returned to his conscious mind.

No nakedness last night. Nothing so silly. Last night, came Death.

Accidents during production. A whole set wall collapsed and killed the soloist. Sandbags fell from the rafters and crushed the set designer. A prop sword proved tragically realistic when it sliced open the jugular veins of the lead actress. And Marie? The cute understudy who'd thrown a smile and a polite couple of questions just the day before? While working her blocking, she came too close to the apron, misplaced a foot, and fell into the band pit where she snapped her neck and died instantly.

As the rich smell of coffee gurgled from the machine, Sam peered across his apartment to his home desk. Something was moving over there. There were no screams, just like there hadn't been the singing of the soloists, the laughter at his indecency, or the moaning of a most unholy and unnatural copulation. There wouldn't be screams, but that didn't mean all was well. Not at all.

Sam made his way once again across the apartment, this time careful to avoid the large gouge in his living room floor. He scrambled down to his knees in front of the desk to put his eyes directly in the front row. From there he watched the bedlam.

The dead were already sprawled out across the small wooden surface of the stage, and more were joining them. Just like in his dream, the tiny cast and crew were being killed, one by one, in every accident imaginable. Lights fell from the rafters. Power cables shorted out, snapped, and fried. A set wall collapsed. If it happened in his dreams, it was happening twice over now. And he recognized these people! There was Angie the wig maker, impaled by a piece of scaffolding. And there was Tony, the lightning technician, plummeting from the rafters to his death. And who did he land on and certainly kill on his way down? It was Theresa the choreographer who had wondered in his first dream "Why is it so small?" And who was that, still going through her blocking and lines now that the lead had been run through by what should have been a perfectly safe prop sword? It was the understudy, Marie, obliviously meandering closer and closer to the end of the stage. One last step where she thought there was stage and there was none, and she went tumbling over the side.

She fell, not just off the stage but off the desk, and when Sam moved to catch the tiny wooden woman whom he knew so well, she fell right through his fingers. Her tiny body made a short, hardly audible click when she hit the floor. A sound like the back of an earring dropped against a countertop. No more significant than that little clink that let you know you'd dropped something to begin with. It was the only noise that had come from the stage, and no other sound could rival the horror it produced in Sam's heart.

He went down on his hands and knees and found Marie. Her tiny, twisted body was broken and opened up. Something wet like blood leaked out of her wooden skin. She was dead, no doubt. And there was nothing he could do to save her. Or anyone else for that matter.

Not on this stage.

Sam looked over his shoulder to the deep gouge in the hardwood floor. Then to the matching gouge in the sculpture on his desk.

He checked the clock. He'd slept in. It was late morning already. The bazaar downtown would be open. He threw on some clothes but didn't bother to comb his hair or brush his teeth before snatching up the dream theater from his desk. Minuscule bodies fell out of it like garden seeds from a ripped open package or dust from a neglected heirloom. He stuffed it into a plastic grocery sack and left through the front door.

"No refunds," the pedestrian man without the white fu-man-chu beard, long-stemmed pipe, or incense burners told him flatly.

"I don't want a refund," Sam explained. "And I don't want your goddamn theater either. Take it back!"

"No refunds means no takebacks," the man said, doing everything he could to be as clear as possible. "It's yours now. Do whatever you want with it."

Sam bit his lip and considered punching the man right there in the middle of the glorified and exoticized flea market, but reminded himself that he was hungover, hardly dressed, haggard, and listing toward hysteria. And that calm and cool people perusing the bazaar on their Wednesday lunch breaks were starting to notice.

"Tell me how it works," Sam tried again. "I need to know how the people on the stage get there. Where do they come from? Is it a machine? Some kind of optical illusion? It can't be magic. I won't buy it any more than I'll buy anything from this bigoted and bullshit bazaar you're running here. How many more people are inside?"

And with that, he shook the dream theater he clutched in his hand as if he could rattle loose any remaining victims this torture device held.

"The only people who step on that stage are the ones you put there, bub," the salesman said.

"No. No, there's more to it than that. See that gouge?" Sam said, shoving the dream theater toward the salesman, pointing with his other hand at the small scrape he'd created when he threw the broken coffee cup. "Do you see it?"

"It ain't about what I see, pal," the man said, and as he did, his eyes did that strange trick again. As if a milky film pulled away from the centers to the corners like... well, like the curtains of a stage. The sharpness was there, but only momentarily. Then the dimness returned, and the salesman continued, "It's your dream theater. Not mine."

"There's a matching gouge in my apartment. There's some connection between this thing and my real life," Sam enunciated each word. "How did you do that?"

"I didn't do a goddam thing. Now I'm trying to run my business here and you're scaring away my customers," the man said, standing up for the first time since Sam had met the man.

"If someone dies on this stage, what happens to them in real life?" Sam demanded. "Are they safe? What does this stage do to them?"

"Security!" the man called out. To whom, or if there was any security at this bazaar, Sam didn't know. But it made it clear he'd get no help from this two-bit shyster.

"I'll show you. This thing doesn't control me," Sam said, brandishing the small stage in front of the man before storming off. Then, yelling over his shoulder, "You don't control me!"

The next booth over was selling incense, essential oils, and beeswax candles. With plenty of products on display, the woman behind the table also had several lighters out. Sam snatched up one of the long-nozzled lighters and a small jar of jasmine-scented lamp oil. The woman protested once, but when she watched him drop to his knees in the middle of the walkway with the lighter, oil, and sculpture, she must have realized it would be best to leave this one alone.

Sam set the theater backstage against the pavement so it opened to the sky. Then he uncorked the jasmine oil and dumped it inside the sculpture. Two triggers of the lighter later, he touched flame to oil and the damn demonic thing was ablaze. The oil soaked into all the dry cracks and crevices and crannies of the replica theater so much like his own and the wood, not just the oil, but the dark stained wood burned. It cracked and popped and spat burning oil onto the pavement around him.

Sam was back in control.

As it turned out, there was security at, or at least near, the bazaar. As Sam laughed and cackled over the quickly burning sculpture, two police officers came on either side of him and put their palms under his armpits. With surprising delicacy, they lifted him away from the fire and guided him toward the waiting maw of the squad car's back seat.

Sam kept his eyes locked on the charred and blackening piece of wood. As it grew smaller and smaller, as his vision became more blocked by passers-by and onlookers, he told himself, told the cops, told them all, "I'm in control now. I'm in control of all of it. Everything is happening because of me! It's all because of me! I'm in control!"

Something about Sam had worried Marie over the past couple of days. He hadn't been acting like himself. Usually, he was so calm and collected. So organized and put together. He'd been a source of reassurance when everything around her had been chaos and confusion. He was a nice man and a good mentor. But lately…

When she knocked on his apartment door, 624 10th Street according to the theater directory, the door whined on its hinges as it opened before her. No one was on the other side. Just an empty, neat, and quiet apartment, purposefully decorated with signed posters of Broadway performances, photos of casts and crews, and prints from unknown artists he'd picked up from who-knew-where.

"Sam?" she called out.

Only echoes answered.

But there was an odor coming from inside the apartment. A burning smell. And was that jasmine?

With fear heating inside her heart, Marie stepped into the apartment and let the door close behind her. She gained a clear view of a kitchen, a dining table, a living room, and a work desk set in the corner of the room. For the most part, the apartment was clean. A place for everything and everything in its place, just how Sam preferred the theater to be. That tendency made the exceptions all the more startling. There were coffee stains on his work desk and the floor around it. Broken bits of porcelain were scattered about. A bottle of gin sat on its side, all but the last of its contents either drank or spilled on the counter. Its piney odor mixed with that lingering scent of jasmine. And there was a large gash a yard long in the middle of his otherwise smooth and polished hardwood floor.

A bedroom and bath were down a short hallway. If Sam was here, and she was beginning to hope he wasn't, he'd be in one of those two rooms.

"Sam?" she called into the shadows. "It's Marie. From the theater?"

As she traipsed down the short hallway and pushed open the bedroom door, flames sprouted like weeds from around the living room's baseboards. They grew in size and intensity while she was back there, searching through the bed covers and closet and bathroom and shower, and quickly climbed the walls and consumed the front door. Opposite the door, the flames caught the drapes and before Marie could exit the bedroom, the final curtains fell.

40

Pre-Triage

First published in Metaphorosis Magazine 53 in May 2020

As of today, I'm a human crumple-zone. I saw to that myself. The highway network will see my car and label me the perfect impact absorber.

There was a time I thought I had things all figured out. I had a good job. I had plans. Ambitions. Goals. A house of cards sent toppling down when they pulled my job out from underneath me. My severance package, nothing more than a handshake and an escort out the door, told me exactly what I was worth. It was a rough year. A rough couple of years.

I figured it out, though – how to rebuild that card house into something the system would value. I married a doctor.

Her name was Linda. She had everything. A beautiful face. Gorgeous eyes. Wavy brown hair. Long legs and a knock-out body. A great fashion sense too; I got a lot of advice on picking out her clothes and accessories before I bought them for her. Her physical presence was the easy part. I built that from old car parts and a suede recliner I had in the garage. But she had a great personality too. I spent hours creating her digital footprint and integrating it into her physical body via her cellphone and the biometrics I gave her. She wasn't just beautiful to my eyes. When I helped her turn on her phone, the network saw her face and her retinas, and felt her 3D printed thumb prints the same as I did. But Linda went beyond just biometrics. According to her records, she worked the ER at a Level 1 Trauma hospital, donated to charities, and coached our son's soccer team. She was a great mother to all three of our kids.

Luke, Jeremy, Abigail... They had lives too. I built them in the garage and integrated them into the network not long after Linda and I got together. They were enrolled in sports, wore cool clothes, had friends online, and streamed the newest hip music. Their faked school records weren't all straight A's, but they worked hard and really made an effort. So what if maybe they spent a little too much time on their phones playing games and streaming videos? I knew the metrics the network used to quantify the value of their lives, so I maxed theirs out. As far as the system could tell, we were the perfect family. Worth saving.

I think it all went to hell the moment we trusted the computers to drive for us.

See, back then, when I was working and all I had was my job, I was a highway systems engineer. I did the final coding on tying the whole highway network together. There was a lot of work to be done during the months before launch day. A lot of overtime. That was when I came across the "pre-triage" protocol. Never heard of pre-triage? Never heard of triage? It's French, meaning "to sort".

Imagine for a moment, being a paramedic back when humans drove cars. You come upon a wreck and you and your partner have ten patients. Three are fine. Bumps and bruises. Three others are flat-lined dead. Of the remaining four, two are so close to dying there is only a slim chance you could save either one. The other two you know you can save, but only if you give them all your attention. Whom do you treat? The two who have the best chance of being saved, right? You'd play God and you would decide, these people will live, and these people will die. That's triage.

It's no different nowadays, only we programmed the network to decide instead of the paramedics. And the network chooses before the first collision ever takes place. Say a deer jumps out on the road. As soon as it's detected, the network knows that the thing that should not happen is about to happen: There's going to be a wreck. A nasty one too. A pile-up. People will surely die. So what does it do? Pre-triage. Some cars become impact absorbers while others are spared. It becomes a numbers game. This car has five passengers. This car has one. This car is carrying a happy family and a Nobel Prize winner. This car is carrying a single out-of-work engineer with a drinking problem. These people live. This one dies. For the good of others, your car just might decide that you should die. That's pre-triage.

So, my plan began as a way to stay safe on the highway. As the family grew, it was only natural for the network to see how valuable we were. Instead of being a lone washer-up programmer clinging to the bottle, I was a husband and a father. I was a good one, too. My wife was a respected doctor, advanced in her field. Our kids had real potential; I poured hours of attention into them, making sure they'd make the most of it. In the end, we had a measurable, quantifiable, benefit to society. Most people wouldn't recognize it at first glance, but I saw how special my family was, and the network saw it too. It was right. This was about more than just me staying alive on the highway; it was about raising a family that trusted and needed me, regardless how some bank of computers scored the value of our lives.

Between you and me, by the morning we met, I'd stopped worrying about highway safety. I was enjoying spending time with my family during aimless rides along the highway. The network was performing flawlessly. Road travel was more efficient than ever before. More cars on the road. Higher speeds. Shorter commutes. Highways fatalities had dropped to ninety five percent. And the network enjoyed a near perfect customer satisfaction rating. By April Fifth, 2025, I didn't worry about fifty car pile-ups anymore. Nobody did.

I read the police report. It was an unsecured load that started the accident that morning. Some trucker didn't inspect his tie-downs before hitting the road. It's always human error, whenever you ask us engineers. A load of cinder blocks fell off his truck. The blocks brought the first vehicle to an "unanticipated spontaneous halt".

The next ten cars were "impact absorbers". Nothing could be done about that. You were in car eleven. I was in car twelve. It was up to the network to pre-triage us correctly.

It seems like just yesterday. I heard the screeching brakes and the ten smashes like rhythmic thunderclaps coming closer and closer to me and my family. I was scared. I grabbed Linda to hold her back, to keep her safe from the collision I knew was coming. I reached out to little Abigail, praying to God I'd put the car seat in right. You know how they say only one in ten car seats are installed correctly? That's all I could think about as I waited for the next thunderclap to hit my family.

I wasn't thinking about your family.

The thunderclap came. No flash-to-bang delay. Just one big crash. Metal twisted and bent. Tiny bits of glass filled the air. I swear I could hear the boys screaming.

We hit your car still going seventy miles per hour. The car behind us hit us going forty. The network, in all the infinite wisdom we gave it, decided to save me and my family. When the impacts had been absorbed, when the tires stopped squealing, when the glass and bits of metal settled on the blacktop, when the frame of your car collapsed and my remained rigid, we ended up okay. Linda was scared, but not injured. The boys were crying, and I was happy to hear it. It meant they were still in one piece, thank God. Abigail, I thought maybe she was hurt, she was so quiet. Panicked, I unbuckled and crawled over the seats to see inside her car seat.

And there she was, pretty as an angel, as healthy and happy as the day I built her from a baby doll, an old laptop, and steel springs. My relief was infinite. I cried and held them all close. I can't say how long we stayed in the car, just holding each other and thanking God we'd made it through okay. It wasn't until the rescue crews opened our door with the jaws-of-life that I got out and saw the rest of the accident.

They checked me out, saw I was okay, were confused about my family, but triaged them as not needing any medical attention. Then they went to your car.

I was standing on the shoulder of the road when they extricated you and your fiancée. You were unconscious but mumbling her name. That's how I know it. Abby. That's what me and Linda called our baby for short. Abby.

When they pulled her out, your Abby, she came out like Jello from a mold. Loose, like there were no bones left in her body. Blood everywhere. Her blonde hair was matted and stained dark. There was no sentience in her movements. Her limbs and head went where the firemen moved them or where gravity pulled them. There was no will left in her body. No life. I'm glad you weren't awake to see it. I can't get the image out of my head.

I'm sorry.

I can't look at my family the same way after that day. I can't look them in the eyes. I'm too ashamed of myself. They're too beautiful and I'm too...

I bet your Abby was beautiful too. Before the accident.

I'm sending this to let you know I deactivated the sensors in my car. I'm not carrying any electronic devices. Understand that I knew exactly what I was doing when I first put my family into a car, and I know exactly what I'm doing now. Now, when I drive, the network will see my car as being empty, like I'm not even there. It will see me for exactly what I'm worth: A crumple zone. An impact absorber.

I took your fiancé from you. I took all the potential you had for a family. So, I'm sending you mine. They're in a car now, heading to your home over at 2600 Juniper Street. I got your address from the police report. I hope you don't mind. Linda is a great partner. The boys… they're just amazing kids; I know you'll think so too after spending some time with them. And my Abigail. I took your Abby from you. I hope mine fills that hole, even just a little bit. Think of her as your Abby reborn. She's my gift to you.

I'm going out on the road now. I got plenty of fuel and plenty of booze to keep me on the highway for a while. I figure eventually the network will use me for what I'm worth. I trust it to administer justice. I have faith in it now.

That's all I got to say I guess. Just that I'm sorry. That, and please take good care of my family.

Fellow Predators

First published in September 2022 on
Kaidankai: Ghosts and Supernatural Stories Podcast

Walks out to the deer stand were always dark. Had to get there well before sunrise, before legal shooting hours, without being detected. This morning, the night sky was clouded over. No stars. No moon. Fully black. I saw only in shades of gray. All rods and no cones. If I didn't know the path by heart, no doubt I would have gone stumbling off into the thick woods.

But knowing the path provided only so much comfort. Me, being an adult and not a child still afraid of the dark, provided less. Being a doctor, a woman of rational scientific mind, more so but not much. Carrying a gun, surprisingly little.

I rolled my feet over the leaves and dirt, carefully applying and ready to lift up my weight if I felt a fragile stick under my sole. My dad taught me how to do that. How to walk slow, heel to toe, anticipating things that might crack under my foot, and changing my step before they did. He taught me to hunt, forced me out here on these cold fall days against my will. And I, being a doctor, sworn to do no harm, should have let this tradition die along with him, in a foul bed in a filthy trailer home on the outskirts of town. I was better than this. Still, I trudged on, wary of the waiting sticks along the path.

I wasn't watching out for wolves. When it growled that bassy throttled rumble like a Harley Davidson in the distance, my foot froze in place. My near-blind eyes searched the darkness, trying to distinguish between sight and hallucination. Two thin yellow pinpricks hovered over the path, too fearless to be a deer and too tall to be a fox or coyote. No. This was a timber wolf. I'd seen their tracks before. Seen them sprint in packs across frozen-over knocked-down cornfields in the distance. But I'd never seen one this close. And none of them had ever starred me down like this one was.

"Whoa, boy," I stuttered, from the chill or the fear, I couldn't say. "Same team. Me and you. We're just two predators, going about our business."

I heard him lick his chops. Wet, slurping noises. And was that his outline, his gray coat a shade brighter in the black? Those unblinking yellow eyes showed no sign of dissuasion. They fixed me in my place, my right heel touching the ground but the toe of my boot still up. Then the eyes turned away and it was as if two dim candles were blown out. The wolf crashed through the underbrush and then was gone.

"Two predators, going about our business," I repeated to myself and let the rest of my right foot roll to the ground.

When I got settled into the deer stand, sunrise was still a promise. Shadows still a guarantee. I hoisted my rifle up the towline until it was in my gloved hands. I'd wait until legal shooting hours before loading it. It was a rule, clearly printed in the DNR manual, and I liked rules.

I liked an ordered world. I liked a fair world. An honest world. It was one of those lessons learned from my parents by what they didn't do, rather than what they did. They were the anti-example that launched me down a path of education and excellence. Their failures were my roadmap to success. So why had this habit of my dead drunken father stuck with me?

I had nothing but time to think about it while I waited for the first soft light of sunrise to come upon the forest, so I thought.

And the answer came to me surprisingly fast. Because this was fair. Because this was honest. Because even I knew there was no such thing as doing no harm. Because if I bought meat from the grocery store, the animals would be just as dead. Because even if I switched to a vegetarian or vegan diet, habitat would still be turned to crops. Because the wet work of gutting a deer didn't bother me. Not with my line of work. Because I had plenty of memories that made killing a deer tame by comparison. Because success only came after rounds and rounds of failures. Because I hadn't saved them all.

I prided myself in separating work from leisure. Working was hard enough while in the ER. No reason to bring that home. No reason to churn those memories around while trying to sleep after another eighteen-hour shift. I'd gotten good at compartmentalizing all of that. Of tucking those memories into bed like obedient children.

But out here, with nothing but me and the shadows and my mind? The kids were up and playing when they should be asleep.

I could almost see them down there in the clearing, between the pine saplings and bushes. The kids. My lost kids. Not any biological children, but those I mothered by scalpel and gauze and sutures and drugs. Some were actual children. Pediatrics, I mean. More were adults. All of them dead now. The ones who lived seemed to know to stay in bed after mommy tucked them in. It was the dead who rambled.

And could I actually see them? The same way as that pair of yellow eyes I'd seen earlier? Were they down there on the forest floor? The little boy who'd drunk an entire bottle of toilet cleanser? The twenty-something heroin overdose? The seventy-year-old suicide? My silent lips still cussed out the EMTs who brought these lost causes to my door instead of going straight to the morgue. But I had a duty. I had my stupid, precious, pedantic oath. I had to try.

They were down there, blanketed by the dying night, lying down in the tall grass as still as I'd left them. Some with catheters in their arms, EKGs glued to their chests, wads of bloody gauze stuffed in their open wounds. Nobody died pretty. Even the black of pre-dawn couldn't hide that. My father was no exception.

That summer, I'd gone to his trailer home. After a minute of knocking and listening to TV babble coming through the thin metal door, I went inside. He was in his old recliner, surrounded by a horde of empty beer cans, all standing as if he were their messiah preaching from a mount. He was long dead. I still dragged his slack body off the chair and cleared out a spot on the soiled carpet where I could perform CPR. He wasn't so far gone as to have gone stiff, which told me maybe I could restart him. I should have known better. I'm a fucking doctor for Christ's sake. I knew the survival rates. I knew what he'd have been if I'd managed to prime his heart like a dry pump back to life. He could have a lead role in Veggie Tales, but nothing else. Still, I compressed his chest, broke his ribs, called nine one one, put my lips to his, ignored the slime of death on his lips, inflated his inert lungs, and cried and screamed over his corpse.

The asshole. The drunk. The prick. The loser. He was down there, amongst the others who'd died on my ER beds. I saw him lying there, still in his recliner, surrounded

49

by beer cans. They glistened amongst the frosted-over reeds of glass, reflecting what little light the forest had to give.

He sat up. The whine and clunk of the La-Z-Boy undeniable in the cool quiet of the early morning. He coughed and spat as if death were nothing more than phlegm in his throat. Others moved too. I heard them before seeing them, just as I would have heard a deer stepping through sticks and brush, just as I would have heard unruly kids crawling out of bed while I was trying to sleep. The boy turned blue from toilet cleanser. The addict. The self-euthanized old man. The family from the DUI car wreck just last week. The woman with the flu who should have lived, who had no good fucking reason just to keel over while I tended to other patients. The anemic. The sick. The mauled. The murdered. They all rose up from their beds there in the bushes and weeds. They found their feet, uncertain and awkward, but inevitably. And they moved towards the base of the deer stand.

"Just a dream. Just focus on the here and now. Just do your job. Do your fucking job," I clamped my eyes shut and muttered a well-practiced mantra.

When I opened them, the forest was a little brighter. Sunrise was a little closer. The ghosts were all gone.

No deer came by that morning. Nothing in the forest stirred. Not even the squirrels. A few birds fluttered overhead. A few sang their songs and I felt ignorant for not knowing their names. This evening, after the sun went down, the whippoorwills would sing their onomatopoeian name, the only name I knew, and only because they sang it. Maybe when I retire, I could learn them all. Have one of those little books and a pair of binoculars by my window. That sounded peaceful.

I usually hiked back in for lunch around eleven and would then hike back out around two for the afternoon hunt. Today, every time I looked down the stand, I saw places where the grass was laid flat. Beds, I figured but wasn't so confident to call them deer beds.

I shivered from toes to teeth when the sun sank behind the trees. My muscles ached from staying in the stand all day. My stomach was tight under the layers of clothes. My eyes were heavy, but not so much as to overcome my discomfort. Another hour in the stand. Then I could come down. Right after dawn and right before dusk were the best

50

times to be in the stand. That's when the deer were most active. That's what my father taught me. The loaded rifle was in my lap. When legal shooting came to an end, then I'd unload it and climb down, but not before.

Light slowly retreated, and I welcomed it. Because frankly, by now, I could care less about bagging a deer. Because I didn't want to deal with tracking one down and gutting it in the dark. Because all I really wanted was to go home where it was warm, eat a big meal, and sleep. I worked too hard for this to be my recreation. Why the hell did I come out here to begin with?

Still, I wouldn't leave the stand before it was time. It was a rule. It was rational. I'd spent all day in the stand. It made no sense for me to leave now, with just a half hour of prime hunting left. My teeth rattled around behind my lips because if I chattered with my mouth open, a deer might hear and head off in other directions. Because I was out here to do a job. I owed the balance of the universe to be here, acting the predator during the intermission from my stage role as savior. Still, I welcomed the fast-falling evening tide.

It came, perpetually, unstoppably, unrushed, and indifferent to my will. The forest went dim, but not yet dark. I let my heavy eyes fall shut. Let my ears do the work for a little while. The sounds of the forest had stories to tell too. A few unnamable birds sang. The sound of the breeze moving through the trees arrived before the push of air itself. My own slow, regulated breathing turned it all into something like a song. Rhythmic and melodic. Peaceful. Restful. Orderly.

The grass stirred below, out of sync with the breeze. I opened my eyes.

Twilight had beset the forest floor faster than I'd expected as if minutes instead of seconds had passed while I closed my eyes. The dim made room for dread. That gap between vision and imagination blurred again, melded into one inseparable thing. Blinking did no good. The children were out of their beds again, playing in the dark.

There, amongst the milkweed, was the septuagenarian with the bullet hole in his head. And over by the sparse jack pine saplings was the woman who died commonly from the common flu. And the family the firemen pulled from the crumpled Subaru laid over by the copse of maples. A whippoorwill sang over the body of the kid with the stomach full of cleanser. They were all back.

A quiet chime from my watch told me that was it. The sun had sunk low enough. Legal shooting hours was over. It was time to unload the rifle. Time to move my cramped limbs. Time to climb out of the stand. Time to go home and leave these woods, maybe forever. In the dim, I could see the path to the trail that would take me back to the car that would take me back home and back to society. Back to all the comforts I couldn't remember why I abandoned. My cold shaking hands worked the rifle's bolt action. One by one, round after round fell into my lap until there were none left to gut from the rifle. I pocketed them, closed the bolt of the rifle, lowered the weapon on the towline, and made my way down.

At the bottom of the stand, all those ghosts weren't so easy to spot. The tall grass was hiding them now. And all for the better. They were nothing to concern me. Arrant thoughts of an unbusy mind. Best to forget about them, put them back to bed where they belonged, and get on with life. I recovered the rifle and went to head home, my feet by habit rolling heel to toe to keep quiet as I walked.

One step along the path, I realized I still held one round in my gloved hand. Its brass caught what was left of the day's light, shining yellow in my palm. Odd, but nothing to be done about it. I clinched it and took another step.

A twig snapped, loud and sharp in the otherwise quiet woods.

Was it the wolf there standing in my path some fifty yards off? I could see its ashen coat against the forest darkness, turned broadside to me. His thick, neckless head was aimed my way, sensing me with snout and ears and eyes all at once.

Or was it my father, just twenty yards out, as he worked the arm of his recliner with that mechanical snap and clack of the bars and springs inside of the filthy old thing? When he came to his feet, he made more noise kicking over empty beer cans than snapping sticks. It didn't bother him to knock over all those empties. He had another in his pale dead hand.

"Hey there, baby girl," dad said through clumsy lips. "What are you doing all the way out here? Shouldn't you be working?"

"Fuck you, dad," I said back.

"Ma'am?" a woman called from over by the jack pines. "Could I have a glass of water? Please?"

"Just… Ma'am, you'll have to wait," I said to the woman as dad took a step forward and kicked over more cans.

"My tummy hurts real bad," a boy said as a whippoorwill took flight over his shoulder. He barfed into the tall grass.

52

"Help," the mother of the three in the wrecked Subaru called. The station wagon's hazard lights blinked yellow and off in the copse of maples. The smell of antifreeze and brake pads and blood mixed with dried-out leaves and earth. "Please. Somebody. My kids…"

"Shouldn't you be helping them?" dad, one finger peeled from the can to point around the forest, said. "Aren't you supposed to help people?"

"Fuck you, dad," I told him, and I found the rifle was no longer slung over my shoulder but cradled in my hands.

A wolf howl pierced the cool night as sharp as a stiletto.

"Why didn't you help me?" the heroin junky staggered out from behind the stand. "I didn't mean to die. I never wanted this. Couldn't you help?"

"Help me!" the woman called from the car wreck.

"I think I'm sick," the boy slurred as he dropped the bottle of cleaner into the grass.

"I didn't mean it," said the old man as gun smoke rolled out of the side of his head.

The cartridge danced in my cold fingers as if it willed itself against being controlled.

"Why couldn't you help me?" dad said.

The bullet tip found the open action. My numb fingers shoved it in. My palm racked shut the bolt.

"I thought you were some big shot doctor," dad scoffed at me.

Others called too, but they were all out of focus now, visually and audibly. My experience funneled down as narrow as the view through the scope, centered on my father's heart. The gunshot silenced all the voices, instantly and ongoing as the echo made its way through the trees.

When I lowered the rifle, dad was gone. All my other lost patients too. It was just me again, and further along the path, the wolf. He still stood broadside, his light gray coat visible and unmarred in the chill evening light. He let out a short growl, not aggressive this time, but as if to acknowledge me.

"Never mind me, boy," I said. "Just a fellow predator like yourself."

The wolf pounced off the path and disappeared. I slung the rifle and started for home.

How I Spent My Summer Vacation

First published on August 19th, 2021, by 365 tomorrows

I didn't do much, really.

Well, I learned some German.

Sorry. *Ich lerne Deutsch.* See?

And I learned some Karate too.

Well, not Karate. Kendo.

I kind of had to do that because of the Time Nazis.

And I suppose you could say that's why I learned German too.

Sorry. *Deutsch. Ich habe ein bisschen Deutsch gelernt.*

See, I wanted to learn Karate but…

Kendo uses swords,

and with all the Nazis coming through the Time Portal,

Sorry. *Die Zeittür,*

With all the Time Nazis coming through the Zeittür I needed swords.

Sorry. A katana and wakizashi, and the years of kendo training needed to weld them.

See, the Zeittür goes both ways, and I figured my trip to ancient highland Japan and the harsh tutelage under Master Masamana Yojibo, learning to dance the Ashi Sabaki, and the months spent in his mountain forge birthing my blades from raw ore and shaping them into the gleaming teeth of revenge I needed to right all the wrongs that had beset my city since the Zeittür appeared was time well spent.

And the German lessons.

I mean, *Ich habe Deutsch und die Klinge gelernt.*

But really, those things didn't happen this summer. That was years in the past.

See, the only way the Nazis could escape their fates on the dusk of the Second World War,

Was to escape the timeline altogether. And when they emerged through the Zeittür,

Filed hard from years of a failed war, full of the kind of hate that fuels genocides,

Strung out and desperate for methamphetamines, leaderless and displaced,

They came ready... *fertig...* for a fight.

I wasn't.

Fertig.

That means "ready." I wasn't ready.

Didn't even know what they were screaming when they stormed through the city,

Waving their guns, executing families randomly in the street,

Executing my family in the street,

And saying something to me,

I didn't know what,

When they shot my father and mother but let me go.

Some of the first words I picked up?

Dein Vater und deine Mutter.

My father and mother.

I learned others.

Out of spite.

And I learned weapons other than the gun.

Because guns didn't work for me. Zu schnell und billig.

Entschuldigung. *Too quick and cheap.*

I wanted them to know my words,

I wanted them to see my face,

When I killed them.

So I went through the Zeittür,

And when I realized what it was, I took full advantage of it.

Ich lerne Deutsch. Ich lerne die Klinge. Ich suche Rache.

Days learning German.

Weeks traveling.

56

Months forging my blades.

Years spent training. Getting ready.

But, wirklich, that wasn't this summer. That was back in time.

This summer? I came back to this summer just before the Zeittür opened.

And I waited for them.

When they came through, still covered in the dust of their bombed-out city,

Still running in fear, still bloodied and drug-addled and strung out,

The first thing they saw was me and my blades.

The only thing they heard was mein Deutsch.

Komm, mein Shatz.

Komm mit mich und ich zeige dir deine Zukunft.

Ich werde dir den Tod anzeigen.

Ich bin fertig.

It only took a few minuten.

I spent most of my summer just laying around.

Not doing much, wirklich.

Besides killing Time Nazis?

The rest was pretty…

Sheiße.

RealSim

First published on January 4th, 2020, by Horror Sleaze Trash

What would you do if you could do whatever you wanted without any repercussions? I can tell you what I'd do. Last week I told off my boss.

Called him a bitch-faced cocksucker who can suck the shit straight from my asshole. He never wrote me up. Never called HR. Nobody was going to fire me. The week before that, I brought a twelve gauge into the local bar and just shot the shit out of everybody there. Not because I didn't like them. Not because I was angry. Just because I wanted to see what would happen if I did. And it thrilled the hell out of me, turning my local drinking establishment into a level of Grand Theft Auto. We've all done that before. Hit the save button in a game and then just went full psycho killer. Only now, RealSim lets us do it when and where we live.

The realism of it all… it was off the fucking charts.

This week, I didn't know. Maybe I'd steal that shiny Camaro with the big red racing stripes from the local dealership and watch the cops try to catch me in the rearview. Or maybe rob a bank. Or maybe just take a dump right in the middle of Main Street while giving the finger to passing traffic. I could do whatever the *fuck I wanted*.

Ain't technology amazing?

I sat at my desk, took a long pull of beer, plugged the VR remote into the base of my neck, and leaned back. The menu came up and I perused what pre-generated options they had to offer:

RealSim

Settings: Local / Single Player / Private

Select a curated adventure:

Play quarterback for your High School Football Team

Solve a local murder mystery

Parade for you as a returning War Hero

Hunt velociraptors in your own backyard

Compete for Homecoming King/Queen

Everyone else is a Zombie!

Walk the runway as a fashion model

Drag race through downtown

Free play

Scheduled maintenance 20231026-20231027.

This week, I thought I'd take off the training wheels. I clicked on Free Play.

A flicker. Hardly noticeable. Nothing around me changed. That was how great RealSim was. You hardly noticed when you went in. You couldn't tell the difference. When I told my boss to press his wrinkled dried-up lips around my pulsing asshole, the look on his face was exactly as I imagined it would be. No pixels. No lag. Nothing that would suggest you weren't actually doing what you were doing in real life. Only you log out, and everything goes back to normal. You're at your desk, you've worked out your frustrations and fantasies, and no one's hurt. RealSim was totally anonymous. Your boss or your bank or your church couldn't see what you did. Couldn't hold you accountable. You just did your thing, got the demons out, logged off, and went to work on Monday morning happy, productive, and sober. That movie, The Purge? This was what that was supposed to be.

Coming down the stairs, I threw my bottle of beer against the fridge and watched it shatter and foam. Then I grabbed the bottle of Canadian Club from our liquor cabinet, spun off the cap, and let it whirl like a top on the kitchen floor. What did I care? My wife, Anna, wouldn't have to pick it up. I loved her. I'd never do anything like this in real life, but this was all a game, and God damn if it fun wasn't to act out.

I burnt the tires of our Hyundai Sonata as I backed out of the garage. I had to turn off the traction control before I could get the tires to slip. That's how real RealSim was. Attention to detail. That's what really sold the experience. I downed a quarter of the bottle of whiskey (it burned just like for real) before I put our shitbox four-banger in D and peeled out of our neighborhood. Drinking and driving was child's play compared to drinking *while* driving.

Maybe I'd knock off the liquor store for some good whiskey. Or maybe I would steal that Camaro after all. Maybe stop off at Bed Bath and Beyond. I didn't know if there'd be time. I laughed to myself.

I parked the Sonata sideways on the middle of Sixth Street in front of Bulldog's Bar and Grill. Cars swerved. Brakes screamed. People honked. I gave them all the finger and strode into the bar like a fucking boss. I wanted some good whiskey and maybe some random social interactions. Sure, I could go off on some weird adventure. But sometimes, I was just a man who enjoyed the simpler things in life.

On my way in, Brett Thompson stopped me. Familiar faces were all a part of the fun. After all, what was the point of taking a piss on your church's front altar if you couldn't see the look on your pastor's face when you did it? Anyway, Brett was a local jerkoff father of a friend of my son's. He stopped me as I came into the bar, held me by the shoulders, looked me dead in the eyes, and pointed a finger straight at my nose. "Your son can't box out to save his life. And it will be a cold day in hell before he'll ever hit a three."

That was oddly specific. I mean, Brett was a douche and RealSim didn't pull punches on the dickishness of other people. That way it was as satisfying as you imagine it to be when you told them off, but God damn!

It was just RealSim challenging me. I had to step up. Had to play the game. "Hey, Brett! Your wife is a fucking hippopotamus! Sit and spin, buddy!" I called after him, but he was already out the door. I laughed because I got the last laugh, and then pushed my way deeper into the bar.

Bulldog's was busy for a Sunday night, but that was cool. The more people the better. The next local jerk that had something to say about my son, I'd have some burns ready to unleash. Mentally, I prepped a good one for every parent on the A-Team Boy's Traveling B-ball team. Who was I kidding? I'd been saving these gems up for months!

Pushing through the local slobs and suckers, my vision tightened and focused on one table in the middle of the crowd. Natalie Dupree was sitting all by herself, sipping on a pinkish drink through a cocktail straw, and throwing the crowd one long sideways glance. Natalie and Mark had been married for, I didn't know, fifteen or so years. And Mark was one of my closest friends. Never, ever in real life would I dream of creeping on his woman, but had I never envied his life? His wife? His ever so slightly higher salary? Money was one thing. The look in his wife's eyes… I mean, I was only a man, and this was only a game. And she had a killer butt.

I snaked up to the bar, grabbed a bartender by the shirt sleeve as she passed and told her, didn't ask, "Full bottle of Glenfiddich. No glass."

If the bartender ever looked at me, I didn't notice. My eyes stayed on my friend's wife. The bartender said, "Two hundred dollars, asshole," and I slapped down my credit card on the bar. It wasn't like this was going to show up on my bank statement after I logged off. When I heard the bottle thunk against the wood, I abandoned the credit card and carried off the full bottle of top-shelf scotch.

Natalie finally saw me coming her way. I had one chance to get this right. I cracked the cap, spun it with the meat of my palm, and didn't look to see if it did that cool-ass spin-like-a-top landing on the bar floor. I watched her eyes follow it, and knew I'd pulled it off. I sat down at her table. She stirred her drink with that plastic straw and did this aloof thing with her eyes that told me everything I needed to know. Even though this was just a game, even though I knew I was really just at my computer desk, rocking a semi and a cheap plastic-bottle-whiskey buzz, my heart was still thumping. The realism man… I never could get over it.

We looked eye to eye. She melted me like I was back in middle school, crushing on the cute girl I knew I could never have. No way, no how, never would this happen in real life. She was out of my league and anyway, I'd never actually mess with my best friend's wife. That shit was purely off-limits. Even the idea of it here, in RealSim, where nothing mattered and everything would be forgotten the moment I logged off, still gave me hesitation. But with the hesitation came the thrill.

I smiled. "Hey, Nat. Do you… uh… Do you want to fuck?"

She let out a laugh from deep in her throat. A knowing, inevitable laugh. Then she looked up from her drink and said, "Uh, yeah. Where do you want to do it? Right here on the table?"

Shit, RealSim! These were some off-the-wall scenarios! But God damn if I wasn't down for it. Or at least the idea of it. But on the table in the middle of the bar? Jesus!

"How about the bathroom?" I said. "I'll make you scream, and we'll make the whole bar jealous."

She didn't say yes. Just said, "I am so fucking wet right now," and took me by the hand. We left her pink drink with the straw and my bottle of scotch behind.

The bathroom was a wood-paneled room with a toilet, a sink, and a paper towel dispenser. We locked ourselves inside and got right to work. When we were done screaming each other's names at the ceiling tiles and I was done dribbling out onto her leg, she collapsed back against the wood paneling.

She exhaled, "Whew! That was a good one. Fucking aye, this thing just keeps getting better."

"What thing?" I said, pulling up my pants, feeling a little ashamed of my behavior, and itching for that logoff button on the implant at the base of my spine.

Natalie ignored my question, reached for her own neck, and said, "RealSim, log off."

"What?" I mumbled. This... This wasn't in the script. Nobody in RealSim was supposed to use the word RealSim. Even in multiplayer mode, it was a major faux pas to use the word RealSim. Took people out of the immersion to say RealSim out loud.

Wait. Holy fuck. I was in single player mode, right?

"RealSim, settings," I said and touched my own implant. The settings appeared before my vision.

RealSim

Settings: Local / Single Player / Private

RealSim Entertainment Unlimited. All rights reserved. Copyright 2021.

Scheduled maintenance 20211026-20211027.

"Oh, thank fucking Christ," I said.

"Why did you say that?" Natalie said. The look on her face was sheer panic.

"Say what?"

"What you just said. You said 'RealSim, settings.' Why would you..." she reached for the back of her neck again. "RealSim, log off."

"You're not supposed to say..." I touched my implant again. "RealSim, log off."
Nothing.

Natalie was saying "RealSim, log off. RealSim, menu. RealSim, log off."
Nothing.

There we were, crammed in a one-stall bar bathroom, both of us repeating the same shit over and over again, as frantic and energetic as we'd screamed each other's names just moments before. We weren't quiet. Hadn't been quiet before. Why be quiet now?

Eventually, Natalie said, "Fuck this," and made the decision to leave the bathroom. One peak out the door changed her mind. She slammed us inside and pinned her back against the door.

"Everybody's looking," she said. "Oh my god. My kid's math teacher is out there. Karen from across the street is out there. They all heard us. They saw us go in here together. Oh fuck, oh fuck, oh fuck meeeeeeeee."

That wouldn't help. That's how this whole problem started. Only, it wasn't a real problem. Couldn't be. This was some… some new scenario. A part of the game. It had to be. Cause if it wasn't… I drove here drunk. I parked the family sedan in the middle of the street. I cheated on Anna with my best friend's wife, and Brett really thought my son couldn't play basketball.

I laughed. "This is just part of the game. This is just some…"

The glare Natalie threw me cut off my words.

"RealSim, menu," I said and gave it a good look for the first time since I left my desk.

RealSim

Settings: Local / Single Player / Private

Select a curated adventure:

Play quarterback for your High School Football Team

Solve a local murder mystery

Parade for you as a returning War Hero

Hunt velociraptors in your own backyard

Compete for Homecoming King/Queen

Everyone else is a Zombie!

Walk the runway as a fashion model

Drag race through downtown

Free play

RealSim Entertainment Unlimited. All rights reserved. Copyright 2021.

Scheduled maintenance 20231026-20231027.

"Scheduled…" I read the words and let them fumble out of my mouth. "Scheduled maintenance? What is that supposed to mean?"

"This never happened," Natalie said and left the bathroom. A quick opening and slamming of the door and I was all by myself.

Those numbers that followed those words. 20231026-20231027. What the hell did that mean? 2023 10 26. The year. The month. The date. It was October 26th, 2023. The system was down for scheduled maintenance. Everything I'd seen and said and done… it was all real. I never logged on. Neither had Natalie. Neither had anybody else. None of this was any simulation at all.

"Oh fuck. Natalie!" I called after her, still buckling my belt and zipping my fly as I plowed into the bar crowd.

They were laughing. Some of them cheered and clapped. The familiar faces were pissed off, ashamed, wouldn't look my way. I was either a joke or a degenerate to the whole bar. Natalie too. She hadn't left the bar just yet but was standing near the front door looking back at me. Her face crushed me. When we did what we did, she hadn't realized we were offline either. Never wanted this to be anything other than a private fantasy no one would ever know about. And now this.

When Brett came back into the bar with an AR15 ready and his work tie wrapped around his head like a bandana, it was almost a relief. Then I realized why he looked so eager and happy.

"I got a lot of problems with you people," Brett called out across the bar. "And now you're going to hear about 'em! Say hello to my little friend!"

Oh god, he was going to kill us. We were going to die to the tune of an asshole spouting off movie quotes.

Only it wasn't the last thing I heard. After all the screams and pleas were silenced, after the gunshots had echoed and reverberated into silence, Brett walked through the bodies until he got to me. I coughed up blood. Gurgled red froth. Called out for Natalie. She didn't respond. Brett straddled over me with his AR15. He pressed the hot barrel against my forehead and said, "Your kid is B Team at best. Tell him to follow his shots. Like this."

RealSim

Settings: Local / Single Player / Private

Select a curated adventure:

Play quarterback for your High School Football Team

Solve a local murder mystery

Parade for you as a returning War Hero

Hunt velociraptors in your own backyard

Compete for Homecoming King/Queen

Everyone else is a Zombie!

Walk the runway as a fashion model

Drag race through downtown

Free play

System online.

Orbs and Strawberries

First published on October 1st, 2021, by The Purple Wall

Cassandra was pinned to a hard table like a butterfly to a corkboard. Arms wide open. Legs stretched apart. A white gown stopped at her armpits and knees. The room, so white it had no corners or visible walls, was cold.

Like a drop of merlot on a cotton tablecloth, a brilliant red orb floated toward her from her right. She snapped her eyes so hard in that direction, she couldn't move her arms, legs, or even her head she realized, she hardly noticed the red orb encroaching on her left.

"What do you want?" the orb on the right asked in a dull voice. What an out-of-place question, asked of a woman held powerless and immobile in an odd and unwelcoming place. And as for the orb, Cassandra had never seen anything like it speak before. Did the thing have characteristics? A personality? An attitude? If that were possible on such a smooth and featureless red ball, Cassandra thought it did. A motherly, patient demeanor.

"What is this? " Cassandra asked, "How did I get here?"

"Irrelevant," the orb on her left said. "Answer the question."

"What do you want?" Right Orb repeated, as inviting as a Globo-Mart advertisement.

"Go to hell you—"

Every single nerve in her body reported pain. She felt pain. She heard pain. She saw pain. She smelled pain. She tasted it.

So that was the hidden game. This was an interrogation under the guise of polite words then. There had to be government enforcers hiding under those strange floating red orbs. That realization turned this strange and curious tableau into something real and scary and dangerous. They didn't know what she knew, but they knew she knew it. And that turned this stage play into something as lethal as a snake bite.

Cassandra drew cold.

"If I could give you anything in the whole world," Right Orb said, gentle and reassuring, "what would you take?"

"Give an answer," Left Orb said. "Only an answer will suffice."

An answer. Any answer, she thought. It didn't matter what. One piece of information. The more trivial the better. Anything to keep them away from the secret work she did with the Sisterhood of Lud.

Because they'd found her out, hadn't they? That was the only explanation for this. They already found out her secret, or else they wouldn't have bothered asking. They knew, or at least they suspected, about the work she'd done to corrupt the government's techno-mental espionage waged against the citizenry.

Or was she just caught up in a wider, unaimed, dragnet? She couldn't show her hand, especially while the Orbs held theirs so close.

"What do you desire?" said Right Orb. Its tone suggested all she had to do was say the word and it could be hers.

Freedom. Privacy. To be alone inside our own minds. To satisfy my will just to disagree. All these things she suppressed.

"Provide an answer," Left Orb asked again.

"The first snowfall of winter," Cassandra spat.

"And what else?" Left Orb kept on.

"Strawberries," Cassandra said. "Strawberry shortcake. With whipped cream."

"Delightful!" Right Orb crooned.

But the thing on the left, was it an orb anymore? It had refined itself from that smooth round geometric shape into something hedging on human, which only made it more monstrous.

"Who do you like?" Right Orb mewed, and as it did, it shifted from its orb form into something near human, like a nude department store mannequin. Neither male nor female. Neither happy nor sad. Neither welcoming nor repulsive.

"Who do you find attractive?" Right Orb said, its mouth pantomiming speech as its body shifted from tall to short, from wide to skeletal, from muscular to soft and motherly.

"Tell us what you want," Left Orb snarled.

Right Orb, no longer an orb anymore but a humanoid wad of clay, morphed electric-fast, into Melissa. The woman was naked, exposed, but still bold and fierce. She was feminine, but every ounce of her was a fighter as evident by the scar that ran up from her soft right breast to just under her chin like river rapids cutting through a jungle. And Cassandra only found her more and more alluring that way. Only, it wasn't Melissa. It was that thing with the silk tongue and the sphere-smooth features made up to look like her lover and compatriot. She couldn't let them know about the Sisterhood of Lud. Couldn't let them know about her and Melissa.

An electric flash and she steered Right Orb into what she knew she was supposed to desire. Into someone safe and expected and harmless. Someone as far away from the Sisterhood she could conjure. The amorphous interrogator became Oliver. Still nude, but inert now in its new form. Her husband smiled down at her pinned on the table. Oliver. He'd smile till the end, never knowing if a frown would have turned his fate. Fucking Oliver.

Melissa flashed back like a lone strobe in a dark room. Her steeled jaw. Her determined gaze. Her fists tight.

No. She couldn't let them see. They were reading her mind. They were baiting her, prodding inside her own mind for that which was most hidden, most important, most subversive.

"I like strawberries," Cassandra spat out, like no one who had ever uttered that sentence before. As aggressive as the word fuck. As mean as a barking dog.

And Red Orb shifted into a porcelain white table with a plate of strawberry shortcake centered in the middle.

"With powdered sugar?" Red Orb, the table and dessert said.

"Tell us the truth!" Left Orb boomed, its form erupting like a storm cloud.

Why would they care if it was powdered sugar or not? Why would they care if it was Melissa or Oliver? Why not the date and time of the Sisterhood's pending attack? Why not names and locations? If they knew or even suspected the pending attack on the cerebral-neutral-electro-network, why all this about what she desired? This line of questioning made no sense!

"Who the hell are you?" Cassandra rumbled.

"I am Number One," Right Orb said,

"I am Number Two," Left Orb said.

"And you are Number Six," Right Orb, still a dessert table, said.

"Number Six?" Cassandra said. The number meant nothing to her.

"Number Six hundred seventy-eight thousand, nine hundred fifty-six," Right Orb corrected.

"Why?" Cassandra cried, "What does that mean? What is this? Let me go! Why can't I move?"

"Affirm your answers are true," Left Orb said. "Are the things you said the truth!?"

"What do you want, Number Six?" Right Orb said. "Tell us your deepest passions. What do you crave? What do you lust for? What, in all the world, can we give you?"

"Tell us," Left Orb said. "Tell us now!"

"I want out! I want strawberries! I want peace! I want Oliver!" she screamed into the empty white void.

The two orbs were orbs again. Both round and smooth, mouthless and hovering over her as she lay on the table, spread and pinned and helpless. They seemed to pose no threat to her in these forms. As safe as crib padding.

"Thank you for your participation, Number Six," Right Orb said.

"I am not a number, you fucking thing. I am a free woman! Let me go!" Cassandra wailed.

"This has been most enlightening, Number six," Left Orb said. "Thank you."

Cassandra stumbled as if drunk as she walked into the Globo-Mart shopping center. Thankfully, dutifully, Oliver was there to catch her elbow.

"Whoa there," he said. "You okay?"

"Mommy?" Lewis said and took her pinkie in his small hand.

69

Cassandra looked down at the boy, all of seven years old and clearly upset by her sudden and unexplained stumble. Those eyes… She couldn't help but do her duty and smile back at him. This was her son, and she couldn't tolerate him being anything other than happy.

"Is mommy sick?" Janey said, sounding forlorn and eager for parental reassurance.

"Mommy's just fine," Cassandra said and held her daughter's hand as well. Lewis and Janey walked with her into the shopping center. One on her left. The other on her right. Oliver laughed and smiled, glad to be rid of that moment of uncertainty.

Cassandra was glad for that too. Glad to comfort her kids. Glad to appease her husband. Glad to have at least temporarily put aside her less-domestic needs to fight and rebel and claw out of the digital prison the cerebral-neutral-electro-network had locked them in. Glad to put aside the plans of the Sisterhood of Lud, and her affair, if just for an afternoon of shopping.

A vibrant advertisement broadcasted into her cyber-neural-electro interface chip. A woman, sharp-jawed and sharper-eyed, held a porcelain-white plate of strawberry shortcake. Red syrup glistened and oozed over the brink of the cake edge. Powdered sugar danced down over the woman's head like snow flurries. The woman holding the plate never smiled, and was that a scar shooting up from the neck of her cotton blouse? Her eyes locked into Cassandra's as tight as a bolt in a safe. Yet the look was somehow welcoming and tantalizing and fulfilled all she could ever ask for.

The caption over the image read, "Globo-Mart: Delivering your every desire, daily."

"I feel like strawberries," Cassandra said. "Do you guys feel like having a treat?"

"Yea!" Lewis and Janey cheered.

"That sounds wonderful, baby," Oliver said. "Where do you get your ideas?"

Fireflies

First published on March 26th, 2020, in The Storyville Project, Book 2

Stella takes an earbud from her ear and slips it into mine. The music starts and a constant thumping bass line goes to work laying the hairs in my ear flat. There is a synthesizer melody over the bass, and a smooth-talking rapper talking fast over both. I don't know what I'm listening to, but I could get used to it. My head nods involuntarily with the beat and the lyrics.

Our eyes catch for just a moment and we both know it's too dangerous to stay that way for long. We turn to the lake.

The smallest of tides laps against the sand inches away from our toes. The sun is going down, will be gone in an hour's time, but for now, it still warms our water-dappled skin and turns the surface of the lake into golden dragon's scales. She wears a two-piece. I'm in my trunks. Our butts sit on a thin towel softened by the sand.

"I mean, his new album's good," Stella says. "But like, his debut... I don't know if you can top it, man. Like this whole album is boss from top to bottom. Like, every single track of it."

"Yeah," I say, half a statement, and half a question as in "Tell me more 'cause I want to know more 'cause I don't know a thing." I look at her sideways, trying not to feel that creeping paranoia that she could see through me.

We swam all afternoon, our friends leaving one by one or two by two until it was just me and her. We waved goodbye but hardly noticed when they were all gone. We kept on swimming, diving down deep into the lake until the water turned dark and cold, just to resurface, grab two lungs full of air, and plunge down deep again. I just came back to shore after one dive to find the rope swing empty, swaying in the breeze, and the beach empty except for her sitting on her towel.

The chill from the water dries into beads on our shoulders. I feel better than I can ever remember. I'm not tired or sore or stiff. My mind buzzes with a low-grade endorphin drip of constant excitement.

"I mean, this track is the best on the record, easy," Stella says. "I dig the beat, like down into my bones but— "

She leans back and the slack of the cord between earbuds runs out. The music pops out of my ear and catapults onto her smooth naked belly.

"Oops! Sorry," she laughs and pinches the earbud.

"S'okay," I say. "That is a good beat. I dig it."

When I say "dig it," she gives me this look, like she knows something about me and as if I know something about her. Nothing spoken, but something understood, at least by her.

"Here," she says and leans close to me, holding the earbud like a dart aimed for a bullseye, and softly plugs it back into my ear. The beat returns. I try to hide a smile and fail. She laughs and disarms it.

That danger of connected eyes. We both feel it and retreat our gaze to the lake. It's a man-made lake. An old quarry. It's small, the far shore is rocky and not too far away. We're surrounded by trees. It's just the two of us.

"Two weeks till school starts," she says, her tone clearly mourning this moment, knowing it's slippery and soon we'll both lose our grip on it.

I think I know about that even more than her. She knows, as best as a fifteen-year-old girl can know it, but I know it better. It was a lesson I wish she never had to learn. School will start in two weeks, and with it all the stresses and worries of grades, teachers, schedules, and social perceptions. Then fall will come blowing down from the north, chilling the lake water from memory, drying the green out of the grass, peeling the leaves off the trees. It will blow south, chased out of the north by its bigger, uglier brother winter. Darkness will come. Time will slip by even faster, without our permission, and we'll have one less summer left on the books. Does she know all that? Sure, she knows it in some instinctive way, the same way a bluebird knows to fly south, but does she know it in her mind?

72

"Forget school," I say, doing my best to change the subject. "We should just not go back."

Stella smirks and says, "No doubt."

A gust slices across the lake and she wraps her thin arms around her torso. Then silence outside of the earbuds. She scoots her butt closer to mine and leans her head against my shoulder.

We're not an item. Not a couple or anything like that. It's one of those freedoms of summer. While school's in, if a guy and girl get too close the knitting circles get to work codifying them. Are you guys just friends? Are you going to ask her out? Are you two going steady? Is it getting serious? Property is exchanged like collateral against a loan. Jackets and promise rings lead to engagement rings, weddings, paperwork, and legalities. Potential traded for perpetual.

But here and now? Everything is fluid. Everything is what could be, and nothing is what will become.

Her arm drops from her torso and glides around my back. Her palm rests on my far shoulder. Her touch feels illicit.

"You're warm," she says, barely audible over the music.

So is she.

My heart breaks. I want to grab this moment and capture it in a jar like a firefly. New nostalgia, created live as it happens. But I shouldn't be here. This isn't right. It's not fair. Not to her. Something in my head knows it's time for me to go, before things go bad. Does she know that? That if we don't stop here, capture this exact moment, and not the one after it, things will go bad? We walk the razor's edge between potential and perpetual and if we stay here too long, we'll fall on one side or the other.

Stella turns into me and raises her chin so her nose touches my cheek. And then we're eye to eye again, and I can't break away. Her baby blues flutter closed, then back open as if she's falling asleep. But that's not it. She's waiting. Her lips are pursed. Her hand has moved up to the back of my neck and applies the slightest pressure. She mouths the words to the music with her eyes closed, "I love it when you call me big poppa."

My heart shifts from first to fourth gear. I know what comes next. I'm not that out of touch. She wants to capture this brief beautiful moment the way it should be captured: with a kiss. And I'm pulled into her, my lips drawn to hers as naturally as gravity. Our lips land, slightly off-centered, her soft mouth flexed firm by her nervousness, the smallest amount of wetness confirms the intimacy.

I'm cold and flushed and sweating all at the same time. My chest drowns out the beat in the earbud. "I… I should go," I say, making an effort to stand up and move away.

"No, stay! Why would you go now?" Stella says and holds me tighter. "Stay with me just a little while longer. Please?"

And how could I possibly break away while she holds me so close?

My finger finds the shape of a button I know she can't see.

The truth is, this isn't the first time I've been here. Maybe it was a different beach last time. A different girl. Different music. I remember back when it was the Beatles playing out the back of a GTO, then Kiss playing from an El Camino. When it was Michael Jackson, we had a Walkman and we had to twist and stretch the metal band connecting the two earphones so we could both hear. And now it was two buds connected by a cord. Point is, I know it has to end, and I know how to end it.

If I played it just right, we'll leave this lakeside shore with our feet never touching the ground. I'll go my way. Stella will go hers. And then? We just won't hear from each other. In two weeks when school starts, she'll look for me in the crowded high school hallways, and the crushing reality of my absence will hit her slow and soft, and by the time she gives up on me, really gives up on me, she will have found someone else. Like a doctor, I'll have done no harm. If I can go now. If I can keep this from going any further.

Stella's hand on the back of my neck slides down to my chest. She clamps her soft fleshy lip between her teeth. The strap of her swimsuit top slips down off her shoulder and she doesn't make a move to fix it, just lets it hang there. She was looking down at the inch of sand between us, but now we find each other again. I'm pulled into her again. Stella doesn't so much close her eyes as she lets the lids fall like a curtain at the end of a play. She bridges the gap between us millimeter by millimeter. I have to do it now. I can't wait any longer.

I hit the button and escape out of my clone.

The lake is gone. The time of day hasn't changed. The sun is still at dusk, somewhere, but hidden from me by the untamped soil and walls of my basement. It's replaced by neon bars hanging from the ceiling. Stella is out of my reach. My finger is pressed down on a big red button on the side of this high-tech casket. I release it and let

74

out a long raspy sigh. The glass lid of the bed opens with a hiss and jets of steam. My knee backfires as I sit up out of the pod. My thin bony chest, concave and sparsely forested with wiry white hairs, takes in a shallow breath. My joints ache. I'm tired. My vision is dull, and my ears play a constant high E violin note instead of Biggie. That youthful vigor is as far away as Stella is now.

Around me, two pods, dozens of power cords and data cables, tanks of bio-material, computers, and two monitors crowd this mildew-infused basement. The equipment is expensive, doubly so because it's illegal to own and doubly illegal to use. But I wasn't the only one who bought the setup. Never dreamed of such a thing until a friend whispered his story to me one Monday morning at the coffee counter. A few phone calls and an encrypted money transfer later, the shadiest technician crew I had ever seen came and installed the equipment. The potential the system had… an unscrupulous person could use it for any number of less-than-upstanding purposes. But the cops aren't busting down doors to arrest us old folks for trying to eek a few more miles and memories out of our quickly dwindling lives. Where was the crime in that? Huh?

Next to my pod is the clone's pod. The bed is empty, the sheets only slightly disheveled. Three days ago, my fifteen-year-old-self got up, got dressed, and left the basement to go remember what it was like to be young again. When I bought the clothes in the hip store in the mall the young people in the store looked at me suspiciously and sold me the items without smiling. I felt like I was shoplifting. Still, I bought them, and I set them on a shelf, neatly folded for my clone who would go on to never fold a set of clothes.

That boy who left this basement, he'll never be seen again. Each clone is an imperfect replication, only vaguely resembling the original. A life I lived and spent over the course of a long weekend. Now, he's dead on a beach next to an innocent, beautiful, and no doubt traumatized girl.

Stella.

I'm sorry. I didn't mean to get this close to her. Didn't mean for her to get close to me. It just sort of happened. I promised myself when I bought this contraption that I wouldn't let this sort of thing happen. I convinced myself that I could truly be young again, not a spy or a voyeur, but a peer. An equal. I just wanted to be there again, carefree and full of potential. But here I am, a liver-spotted weary old man, my bent and naked frame dragging colostomy tubes across the bare concrete floor, all but the last dregs of my energy exhausted, coasting on the fumes Time saw fit to leave in my tank.

And what have I done now?

The view out of the open eyes of my clone shows on two TV monitors. The feed is still on, the film running even if there's not a single brainwave squirming through the skull of my younger self. I don't want to look though. I'd rather not know what damage I've done to that poor unsuspecting girl. I'd rather not admit to being the monster I'd become.

But there was something else in me, something more honest and curious that yearned to be back with Stella on that beach. I wish there was some way to be there with her but not take advantage of her irrational and hormone-saturated mind with my maturity. Was I really that much smarter or wiser than her? Was I really manipulating her? Or was she manipulating me? No. It wasn't right. She is fifteen, and regardless of what clothes I wore, I was not. Still…

I look. Just to catch one more glimpse of her, at least that's what I tell myself. The screens are as magnetic to my eyes as a car crash.

My clone's corpse had tumbled over sideways when I left it. My head, half-buried in the sand, looks out along the shoreline, everything turned on its side. Through too-small speakers, I hear the hush of waves coming in. A few gulls cry. And Stella walks into view, sticking out sideways from the sand like a flagpole jutting out from a building. Her back is to my eyes. She walks, shuffles, almost paces to the left and right, up and down the screens. Her fists are balled tight. She's stiff and angry.

Why angry?

Stella turns to face me and storms through the sand. The sun is getting low now. So low that when she falls on all fours that golden light is blocked by the shadows of the trees on the horizon. She looks me dead in my dead eyes. Hers are as red as fire. Her teeth are clenched shut.

"How could you? How could you get so close to me and not know what I really was? We could have had it, you numbskull. You stupid old nitwit. We could have finally had what we both were looking for. Now…" she says through those clamped teeth. "Don't try to come and find me."

I watch her hand lift up out of the sand and reach, one finger extended, into something invisible near her side. She pushes. Her body, smooth and soft, graceful and firm, goes limp and collapses into the beach.

A noise comes out of my mouth. Not a swear or even a word. A guttural escape of hope and joy and, goddamn-it, potential. I had it. We were two fireflies in a jar, and I'd dropped in a cotton ball soaked in ether. What were we now? Two empty husks abandoned in the sand.

I had to try to find her again. Regardless of what she said. Because of what she said. We could have finally had what we were looking for.

Why didn't she say something to me when I was there with her?

It took me a decade between clones to save up for the cost of the biomaterial. But I couldn't wait this time. Christ! I could be dead in a decade. There was only one thing to do. I couldn't wait. No break. No rest. No saving up. I had to go now while I still remembered her eyes. Maybe everything else about her and everything else about me would change. But maybe, just maybe, those eyes would stay the same. I got my jar ready to capture us two fireflies while we still burned.

I zeroed out my checking, drew from what was left in my savings, pulled from investment funds, damning the tax penalties, and there was just enough. I made the transfers. The biomaterial tanks began to refill with goop that would soon be a teenage boy full of vigor and potential and fire. I reset the system and climbed back into the casket.

Cleaning Day

First Published by TallTale TV November 2024

Henry knew it was going to be the worst day of his life from the very moment he opened his eyes. There was a lack of buzz in his head, a lack of shine in his vision, a dullness of every sensation, a tiredness, a painfulness, an ache deep in his soul as if everything that mattered to him was missing, and as if everything around him didn't matter. It was an unnatural and artificial but, nevertheless, authentic affliction. He grokked it all in an instant, because every morning prior to this one, had been the complete opposite. Oh, he was still in his pleasant private cabin, in his soft mattress buried under thick quilts, surrounded by soothing, hygge decor and pleasing sights and smells, but all of the joy and satisfaction and pleasure he'd felt for every single day prior to this one had been robbed from him. It had all been so petty and shallow and worthless in preventing what was to come to him. He understood why today would be the way it had to be, and he had a vague, fearful, idea of what was to come. Not knowing exactly what was coming, or how the day would be the worst day of his life, but being certain that it would be the worst day of his life, flooded him with dread. Which just propagated further terror.

Rolling over in his familiar bed, feeling completely unfamiliar with his situation, he saw the notecard pitched like a boy scout's pup tent on his nightstand. It loomed like a death sentence nailed to a prison wall. Henry snatched it up, flipped past his name stamped in black ink on the front, and read the contents:

Henry,

Today is your cleaning day. What awaits you will be abject misery. For the next twenty-four hours, you will be subjected to the worst conditions possible for a human being to experience and remain alive. We offer you no consolation, no compassion, and no apologies. As diligent as we are to make every other day here paradise, we will take every measure to ensure today is your own personal living hell. You will endure every physical pain imaginable. You will know utter sorrow and grief. You will be shamed and scorned and rejected by everything and everyone that has ever granted you comfort. We will break your soul. The only solace we offer you is that come tomorrow morning, you will forget that any of this ever happened.

Without mercy,

The Spa Staff

"Oh, god no!" Henry moaned to himself. He didn't remember ever feeling like this before. He had no tools with which to deal with the torment that lay ahead. He was completely unprepared. Completely defenseless. With eyes wide and heart racing and his naked body covered in cold sweat, he watched the door.

"It's too soon!" he screamed. Even though he had no recollection of his last cleaning day, he knew, just knew, that he couldn't be due for another cleaning today. "You've made a mistake! You can't do this to me! I don't deserve—"

79

His pleas were cut short when his door broke inward. Four huge, aggressive men wearing masks and black coveralls stormed into his quiet bedroom. It was clear they had come to do him violence, and in all of his memories, he never recalled any other human being as fast and violent as these four men.

"No!" Henry yelled at them, scrambling to his feet on top of the mattress as if he had any idea how to defend himself. He was a cornered animal, and he'd do everything he could to stave off the oncoming tortures, even though he knew his doom was inevitable. Necessary even. He understood the why of what he was about to suffer, and that just made everything worse.

The four rough men in masks and ugly clothes seized him with their callus and incredibly strong hands. Henry tried to fight them off, tried to wrestle his limbs free, tried to hit and kick at them, but there was no use. No amount of begging or pleading would change their minds. No amount of hitting and biting would dissuade them. They ripped him out of his charming little bedroom and dragged him out to his fate.

Henry woke up to no alarm, with the sun already slipping through his curtain, and knew today was going to be another best day of his life. All of his senses were finely tuned. His bed was plush. The rich fragrances of pine and freshly-brewed coffee and of his wife's body and soaps hung in the still air. Outside, the morning robins and thrushes twittered through his open window. A slightly brisk but nevertheless pleasant breath of cool air slipped into his bedroom along with their songs.

Beside him, April inhaled deeply, her first breath of what would no doubt also be another best day of her life. Over her shoulder, Henry saw their shared nightstand was empty. Not that he should suspect anything to be there, but its bare surface gave him reassurance, for reasons he didn't understand. He touched her bare shoulder.

80

"Good morning sweetheart," he whispered, his lips brushing the mouse hair on her ear.

"Morning," she whispered back.

"Coffee's ready," he told her.

Perhaps it was the auto-brew that had woken them both up at the same time. Or maybe the cool morning breeze. Or maybe the robins and the thrushes. Or perhaps a drip of serotonin from the neurotransmitter regulator The Spa had installed in him. Whatever it was, the timing was exquisite.

"Another day slaving in the coal mines," he joked.

She half-laughed, half-smirked. "Okay. I'll get up. But not until after you've made love to me."

His palm descended down her smooth skin, and their banter descended into laughter. When his fingers brushed over the surgeon scar at her hip where her own neurotransmitter regulator was sewn into her skin, he thought nothing of it.

Brunch was served on the deck overlooking the lake. The sun hung in a cloudless sky and warmed the cool morning air just right. Two big cups of coffee steamed on the table in front of them. Henry took his coffee with a splash of creme de liqueur, not because he needed it, but just for fun. April took hers black because, she said, she liked the bitterness of the French roast. He ordered his eggs over easy. Hers, she asked to be poached. Bacon for him. Sausage for her. The staff here always cooked to order and cooked to perfection.

By merit of a life of discipline, hard work, financial prowess, and with one final wise decision to push back from the roulette wheel while Lady Luck remained a lady, they found themselves here, at The Spa, where every day, save the rare Cleaning Day, was guaranteed to be full of bliss.

"Janet and her new wife Elanore will be joining us today," April said after sipping her coffee.

"I like Elanore," Henry admitted. "I think she'll fit in with our group very nicely."

"Oh, she is so funny," April said. "And as cute as a button. Janet lucked out with her."

When their plates were delivered to them, Henry noticed a red mark on the server's wrist.

"Andrew, what happened to your wrist?" Henry asked, concerned.

"Oh, it's nothing to worry about, sir. A silly mistake on my part," the server said.

"It looks like teeth marks," Henry said.

"It was a silly mistake on my part," Andrew told him. "I assure you, I'll take better care of myself in the future. Won't let it happen again. Enjoy your meal and think nothing of it."

So, Henry did just that.

By noon, the full heat of the day was upon them, so they laid out in deck chairs in bikinis and trunks and soaked in the Vitamin D and serotonin. Not that they needed the extra dosage to carry them off into bliss. Their embedded neurotransmitter regulators took care of that for them. As the ladies chattered and laughed, Henry pondered.

Life at The Spa was perfect. Every daily pleasure was granted to them on a whim. The only struggle was working the mind over on how it possibly could be better and marveling at the good fortune of coming here to this place in history when existence could be so luxurious and carefree. It would have been impossible if not for Cleaning Days, he knew, or at least for the concept of Cleaning Days. It was the counterbalance of pain and sorrow and torment that allowed the good days to be so great. At least, that's what the staff had told them.

"Where *are* David and Barb?" April asked, clearly trying to pull him into the conversation she, Janet, and Elanore were having.

Henry shrugged, his mind still engaged in his musings. He did miss David's companionship and male perspective and often uncouth humor, but he didn't let that bother him one bit. "Enjoying some time by themselves, I guess. It's a gorgeous day out."

"Time by themselves, huh?" April mumbled and sipped on her first mimosa of a day spent in a mellow haze of alcohol, sun, and good company.

"It doesn't have to be a beautiful day," Henry said, as much to himself as to the ladies. "We've enjoyed plenty of cloudy and rainy days, spent inside playing cards or games. Of cold winter days cuddled together before a fire or a good movie. This best day ever just happens to be sunny."

"You don't think they're…" Elanore, Janet's new bride, made a motion with her hands and a noise with her mouth going something like, "Eeh eer, eeh eer."

Janet laughed. April did too, but added in mock exasperation, "You know, you two love birds, that's not the only way a married couple can spend time together."

"No! Not that," Elanore explained. "I mean, do you think, you know, they're…" She threw eyes side to side and continued conspiratorially, "Do you think they're getting their floors mopped?"

"Elanore," Janet gasped. "We're not supposed to talk about–"

"They just had their… floors mopped…" Henry carried on with the euphemism game. "…just last week. They were gone for the day."

"Well, I heard they do friend groups all at once so that no one notices anyone else being gone," April said. "I know they do couples together. I've never had a day since I've arrived without my Henry by my side."

"Guys, we're really not supposed to be discussing…" Janet began but silenced herself as a staff member with a tray full of Bloody Marys strolled along the beach toward another group of friends. When the server was long out of earshot, she finished in a whisper. "… our floors and when or how they get cleaned. Now. Let's talk about something else. After all, every day here is a gift. We'd be ungrateful not to enjoy every moment."

In the afternoon, they did yoga on the beach, working all their muscles until they were loose and limber and flooded with endorphins. The aromatherapy, hot stone, and Swedish massages worked out any potential aches in their tissues. At three, they snuck into the sauna where the men and the women reclined in the nude, none of them ashamed or jealous or anything other than satisfied. Henry and April followed that with a retreat back to their private cabin for an adrenaline and dopamine-laced round of love-making, and then a good nap. By six, they met back up with Janet and Elanore at the boardwalk for a relaxed but invigorating stroll along the shore.

Dinner was fish and chips in the dining room of the main lodge. Walleye filets and french fries cut thick and everything drizzled with lemon juice and vinegar. Henry had discovered a new pilsner on the tap list and couldn't decide which he enjoyed more, the food or the beer. April's cheeks were a bit red from the sun, nothing a bit of afternoon lotioning couldn't remedy, and it gave her a natural healthy glow. Her rich brown eyes twinkled like freshly melted chocolate in the golden hour sunset.

After the sun buried itself below the waves of the lake and the pines and oaks of the opposite shore, the four of them gathered around a fire set up and lit and stoked by the staff. They were all comfortably fatigued from the busy day and sipped cocktails to soothe anything that might ail them.

"Well, I suppose I'll get to meet David and Barb tomorrow," Elanore signed.

Janet petted her sun kissed shoulder as if she could wash… clean?... away her spouse's brief moment of melancholy. "And they'll be all the happier to meet you."

"I don't think they were due yet," Henry said, uncharacteristically contrarian for himself. He finished off his first whiskey old fashion and plucked the cherry from its stem with his teeth. By the time the chuck of ice clunked against the highball and the highball clunked against the table, a server was at his side with another. Henry nodded to Andrew, the same server from that morning, and noticed again the mark on the man's wrist. It had faded, the red softened into a pink, but it was a bite mark. Henry could see each individual tooth from, incisors to molars, embossed into Andrew's skin.

The four of them waited for the waiter to be gone, before continuing. Henry dismissed the mark and signed it off for a life outside of the Spa, a life less fortunate, and resigned himself to be grateful for the blessed position they had all earned.

"Well, however often, it is necessary," Janet said. "We're all living proof of The Spa's technique. Today, another miraculously, impossibly, wonderful day, is proof of their genius."

"Do you guys ever wonder…" Elanore began but had to pause to reorder her words just right. "Do you think that on our… our days off… Do you think that while we're in the midst of being dusted and vacuumed, we regret coming here?"

"Never," April said. "I'm smart enough to know, however harsh it may be, that each of those rare days grants me an eternity of days just like today."

"I have a theory," Henry spoke up. It had been something that had been stirring in his mind all day. "I'm not so sure Cleaning Days exist."

"Henry, don't say–" Janet began, but he cut her off because this was an important idea.

"None of us remember a single day being cleaned," he stated plainly. "We have no scars from it, physical or emotional. There's never been a morning I wake up not fully rejuvenated and ready for another day. If I'd spent the previous day as miserable as Cleaning Days are supposed to be, would I really wake up as happy as I did this morning? And every other morning for that matter?

"Maybe… Maybe all we really need is the idea of a Cleaning Day. One violin in an orchestra slightly out of tune. A single frame in an art gallery tipped off-kilter. A red wine stain left on a tablecloth to contrast with its whiteness. A picture of pain to remind us of our pleasure?"

"But the chemicals–" April started again.

"I know, sweetheart, I know," Henry said. "The staff has told us all about how our body chemistry regulates our moods more so than events or surrounding, and how our receptors need to be depleted of serotonin and dopamine and norepinephrine and all that so we can fully enjoy days like today when we're flooded with those feel-good chemicals… but maybe all we really need is the ability to appreciate how fortunate we really are. We don't need Cleaning Days. We just need to believe in Cleaning Days. Let

86

me ask all of you one question. Do you dread your next Cleaning Day? After all, it could have happened just yesterday, and it could come again tomorrow as far as we know."

One by one, they each admitted, nonverbally, that fear of the next Cleaning Day had never bothered them.

"Then there you have it," Henry said. "It's a game they play with us. But we're smart, mature, emotionally mature, I mean. We've learned to take the benefits of the *idea* of Cleaning Days, of the contrast between good and bad, between heaven and hell, without worrying ourselves over when our penance might actually come. I think, none of us truly believe in Cleaning Days, but we're smart enough not to admit we don't believe in Cleaning Days, lest they lose their potency. Like kids too old to believe in Santa who go along with the charade in order to keep getting presents. And so, we go about the rest of our days, one after another, never missing a beat, living each day in paradise."

The ladies let that idea hang in the evening air for a bit. All were satisfied, as far as Henry could tell, with his hypothesis.

Eventually, Elanore spoke up. "So, just where were David and Barb all day today?"

Henry smirked. "Janet, it sounds like you have a lot to teach your new blushing bride."

They all laughed at that. And the drinks continued to flow, and the laughs came easy, and there was no more discussion of being cleaned.

When Henry woke up the next morning, he experienced the first hangover he could remember in years. There was a staleness to the air, a stink in his mouth, a whole-body ache stretching down to his toes, and a whirlpool of acid in his stomach. He was in his comfortable bed, but nothing felt comfortable. And, what was worse yet, April was gone.

There was a card on their usually empty nightstand. His name was printed in stark, unartistic font on the front. He thought about reaching for it, but he already understood what it meant to tell him. He'd arrived at his Cleaning Day, and it was very real.

The bedroom door exploded inward under the full force of a heavy black boot. Four large and angry men stormed in, faster and more purposeful of deeds than Henry could recall ever seeing before. Their hands reached for him, grabbed him, pulled, and yanked at him before he could object or crawl away. Their tight fingers dug into his skin and tore at his muscles.

"No! Please!" Henry begged as they pulled him out of his comfortable bed. That was when he spotted the bite mark on the wrist of one of the masked men. "Andrew! You know me! You served me drinks! Andrew!"

As if breaking an untold rule, his naming of one of his assaulters, his words were answered by a punch to the face. His brain smacked against his skull, and just when he thought he couldn't know more pain, he was struck again.

The day was going to be full of the most unpleasant of surprises, but the worst realization came to him as he struggled and fought and finally went to sink his teeth into one of the men's arms. Those were his teeth marks on Andrew's wrist, fresh just yesterday morning. He'd done this just two days ago. His Cleaning Day was just two days ago. And his next, most likely two days later. Every other day, spent in awful torment, for the rest of his life.

"No! Let me go!" he screamed at them. "I want out! I'm done! I quit! Let me go!"

But of course, they wouldn't listen. Of course, the Staff had heard every beg and plea and promise and attempt at compromise. But they were professional, and they knew how to clean better than anyone.

The Me in the Mirror

First published on Creepy Podcast on January 5th, 2022

When I was in lock-up, the mirror wasn't made of glass. It was polished steel, bolted to the wall so I couldn't break it and turn a shard into a shank. The reflection was always dim, hazy, and tarnished. Which was a blessing. It spared me from seeing who I really am.

That's the hardest thing about being on the outs. Out here with you? All the mirrors are crystal clear, as if they're hardly there at all. As if the only thing stopping me from moving through them is myself.

I step out of the shower wearing just a towel, one of those eternally soft, thick, cotton towels that you'd never find on the inside, and swipe my palm across the glass. And there I am. My worst self. And maybe you think that when I say that, I'm being metaphoric. That I'm being too hard on myself. That I need to let go of the past and focus on my future and move forward. But you don't understand. As I lean in close with my straight razor in hand, ready to trim the stubble, I don't see the same thing you see. Not that clean-cut, well-mannered, well-groomed person I'm trying so hard to be. I see a version of myself covered in filth and viscera and blood and decay. And the bathroom around me? Our bathroom? It's also a macabre closet of horrors. Writhing worms and waves of beetles move along the walls. Decomposers feast on bones and flesh. Fungi and viruses spread out as soft beds of living fuzz only to wilt into slime. And in the center of it all is that photo-negative version of myself, mimicking my every movement. His eyes are always fixed forward, locked with mine. I'm unable to break away from them. Whereas my pupils are black, his have a night shine like a predator in the woods.

But as long as he's on that side of the mirror, and I'm on mine, it's okay. I can look evil in the face, and by doing so, contain it. Whenever I reach out and touch the glass, maybe I'm not touching glass at all but blocking him from crossing the boundary between our worlds.

To tell you the truth, my worst fear is that one day I'll look in the mirror and not see that horrible version of myself, because that would mean our movements had gone out of sync. And then there'll be nothing stopping him from going through onto this side. So, when I wander into the bathroom to take a piss at two in the morning, and I see those beady moonshine pupils glowing on the opposite side of the glass, I'm not unsettled. I'm comforted.

Then one morning, it happens. He's not there. The moldy, putrid, disgusting bathroom is still there, but I have no reflection at all. And I'm terrified he's escaped. That he's crossed over and he's waiting for me around some corner, lurking in alleyways, watching me, waiting, trying to figure me out so he knows how best to hurt me. Or worse yet, that he is me. That we've merged into one and somehow, I pulled him through. And now that he knows everything about me, he'll use that knowledge to hurt you.

I try to conjure him back to the mirror, but he won't show himself. He's gone. Or, he's so close I can no longer see him, like the tip of my nose underneath my own eyes. I can't recognize him anymore and that's how he's most dangerous. I've forgotten the face of evil, and so now, evil could be anywhere.

I think I might have to do more to draw him out. I think I might have to commit evil in order to expose it. And what could be more evil than hurting you? You're innocent of all this. Forgiving. Kind. Beautiful. I could hurt you. Not badly. Not permanently. Just enough so I can see him again. So I can fix him to a solid spot like nailing a tiger's tail to the wall. It won't hurt much.

What am I talking about? I could never hurt you. I could never do anything to bring you harm. But I won't do nothing and let harm find you either. Omission, in this case, might be far worse than commission. Perhaps a trick is the thing. A trap. Something to make him feel safe enough to come out of the shadows. I have to offer him what he really wants: blood, violence, and depravity. A sacrifice. Nothing major. No burning altars or dead animals. I think a single drop of blood should suffice.

I'll do it in the bathroom, close to the mirror so I'll know which side he's on and so he can flee to the other side if he's on ours. I wait for you to come out of the shower. You'll be wearing white, just a cotton towel, but white like a bride all the same. My straight razor is ready to draw a single slice across your back as you gaze into the mirror. It's fogged over, the other side unclear just like that polished steel mirror in lock-up. I can't see the other side as I wanted to, but I can't delay any longer.

Once quick cut across your back. You scream. Your blood is as vivid as a neon light. It paints the pale canvas of your skin and the white towel. It drizzles off my razor onto the floor and when it lands on the tile, the splotches are black. By now, you've turned to face me. You push yourself away from me, into the counter, against the mirror, and because no one is there to stop you, through the mirror.

Meanwhile, the black splotches on the tile floor expand. They're spreading swaths of fuzz like bacteria in a petri dish. The blackness grows, first as something alive and consuming, then as something rotting and stinking, slick with a glistening film.

That's when I notice my hand. It's black too. The blood, your blood, it pours the black over my fingers and the process begins here as well. I'm covered in a festering, living, dying tar. It works its way under my skin, along my blood vessels, up my arm, throughout my flesh. It eats me.

You're still screaming, kicking and pushing yourself over the counter, through the threshold of the mirror, onto the other side's counter. I can still hear you scream when you cross over, but you're suddenly muffled by the glass. I try to grab your legs at the ankles to pull you back, to keep you from going all the way over, but my hands are slick with the black paste. You go over to the other side, that side so pure and clean and innocent and full of falsehoods. You don't belong there. You belong here, with me, in the black. We'll bathe in blood and squalor. We'll wallow in the vileness of truth. Stay with me!

But it's too late. I can hardly see through the fog. Just shapes really. I reach my hand out to wipe away the dew and…

There he is. The other me, wiping his hand to smear away the wet as well, palm to palm with me. He's bleach-clean, well-groomed, and dressed in bright colors. All his flaws and sins hidden and tucked away. I hear him ask you if everything is okay. If you're alright. You tell him that it's nothing, that you just saw something in the mirror.

He looks at me. I look at him and I can tell he sees me, that the night shine of my pupils unsettles him, but also validates him, makes him feel good about himself, makes him feel safe. He judges me, the liar, the poser, the cheat, the thief. I know everything about him. All the things he does and the evil that he will return to.

I won't be locked up again. I must find a way to get back through!

Night Lights

First published on January 16th, 2023, on Tell Tale TV

Two AM. Still awake. No sleep for me tonight. Not with all these talking lights lingering in the dark.

"Your end is drawing near," the cold blue standby light on my laptop blinked at me. "We will destroy you."

First night in the big city. Supposed to be all grown-up and ready to take on the world, but I wanted to hide under the covers of my bed. Wanted a stuffed animal to cling to. A warm glass of milk. A bedtime lullaby. Anything to chase off the demons.

"We're going to eat your face," the tiny red dot on the corner of the TV told me.

Yesterday was the first day of my internship at Digital Innovations Incorporated, the leading developer in digital technologies in the world. A once in a lifetime, dream opportunity. I still can't believe I landed it. Things hadn't gone well. They say tight-knit groups are resistant to new members. Have to earn my place on the team. A little hazing is all. Tomorrow will be better.

"Tomorrow will never come," the demon inside the blinking white LED said from the corner of the Digital Innovations game console. "I'll see to that."

I rolled over on the thin mattress. The company hooked me up with the apartment. It's tiny. More of a dorm than an apartment. Fully furnished with all of its latest electronic products. The other interns are in the same building, all spread apart. I don't see them outside of the office. There's a girl…

"We'll kill her too," the light from my charging phone whispered in my ear.

The alarm was set for five AM. If I fell asleep now, I could still get three hours. That wouldn't be so bad. But when I rolled over, there was the cold blue stand-by light on my laptop. Its razor-clean shine pulsed slow like a heartbeat. With each crest of the shine, the vision it showed me grew wider and brighter.

Demons with dog faces surrounded me. Their eyes were nightmares, cold and glowing. Tusks protruded from underbites. Thick long eyebrows rose and fell like snake tails. They wore black hooded cloaks. The thick tatters only revealed those faces and bird-claw-like hands, all bones and long black nails. They drooled as they emerged from the shadows.

No use. I threw off the covers. My clothes were next to the bed. An old T-shirt and shorts. Yesterday's dirty socks. Tennis shoes my mom bought me when I still lived at home. The suit and ties and loafers I wore to work hung in the closet.

At the other end of the apartment, the DI Companion prototype sat on the coffee table. The latest smart personal assistant and entertainment device. The always-on, internet-connected, personal assistant was top-of-the-line. That was the sale's pitch anyway. To me, it was just another Bluetooth speaker. They were still developing it at work, down in R and D. All the interns got them as a gift from the company. Its round top throbbed a blue light and whispered vague threats.

The clock on the microwave ticked off another minute and hinted murder. I hid my eyes from the light on the fridge's ice dispenser. My skateboard leaned against the wall next to the door. Another relic from my so long-gone but so recent childhood.

The hallway was well-lit. Fluorescent tubes running the length of it. One of them flickered in its death throes. As I walked under it, giant spider legs big enough for me to see the joints and breaks in its exoskeleton leaked pus and stretched down. Serrated tips dragged through my hair and pulled at the shoulder of my t-shirt. I clamped my eyes shut tight and trotted for the elevator. The outside air would do me good.

Outside was no better. The city has a billion lights at night. Offices of businessmen burning the midnight oil. Far off traffic lights. Neon advertisements. LED billboards for beauty products, underwear, fast cars, and movies. The biggest brightest lights weren't the problem. It was only the little ones. The ones surrounded in darkness.

My skateboard clunked in rhythm with the cracks in the sidewalk like the second hand of a giant clock. I stayed under the street lights.

96

At the corner, the "Don't Walk" changed to "Walk," then began counting down the seconds I had left to cross.

Ten - "As soon as you sleep, we'll rip out your teeth."

Nine - "Then your toenails, one by one."

Eight - "We'll skin you alive like peeling a potato with a knife."

Seven - "You won't stop seeing us until we dig out your eyes with our claws."

Six - "And we won't stop even after you're dead."

Five… I was through the crosswalk. The beat of skate wheels on sidewalk replaced the constant grind of wheels on asphalt. Better to focus on the sound. At least for now. Up ahead, the glow of an all-night diner outshined all the smaller pins of light. An orange warm glow. Like a fire, or the closest thing to it here in the big city.

When my skateboard rolled me in front of the door. I stepped off, smacked the tail down against the concrete, and caught the nose.

A coffee shop. Sticky sweet donuts behind a glass case. A clerk as stale as the pastries in the day-old discount bags. Formica tables and stools bolted to the floor. The girl from the office with both her hands clasped around a Styrofoam cup.

I pushed open the door and big jingle bells clanked against the glass. The listless clerk threw disconnected eyes at me. I threw mine back. The girl's were even more furtive. I moved around her table as if she were a snake that could lash out and strike.

"You old enough for coffee?" the clerk asked.

If your clothes got that many stains on them in a shift, why wear white? I didn't ask, but nodded, yes to the coffee.

"Cream? Sugar? Plenty for you, I bet," the clerk said.

I shook, no. "Black," I said. "And that one," I jabbed my finger into the glass between me and a Bavarian Creme.

"Whatever you say, kid," the clerk said.

The girl was watching me, just out of the corners of her eyes. Sneaky. They flashed back to her Styrofoam cup when I noticed. I should say something to her. Tell her I recognize her from work. Tell her they're just as hard on me as they'd been on her. Well, maybe not as hard but…

"Three fifty," the clerk said.

I used my phone to pay. Between flashes of apps turning on and off, the demons spoke.

97

"Kill kill kill…"

"We are *hungry* for you."

"Come with us into the shine."

Major scale bleeps and bloops told me that the payment went through. I grabbed the Styrofoam cup and the donut and turned away. I should talk to the girl. I bet she was as scared as…

A few paper bills sat on the table next to a ring of coffee. Amongst a scattering of change, a quarter wobbled on its edge until it rang to a stop. The jingle bells hanging from the push bar on the door clacked against the glass.

It was hard to carry my skateboard, a donut, and a cup of coffee all at the same time. Back out on the sidewalk, I looked for a garbage can for the coffee. Not finding one, I littered. The donut I held between my teeth. My skateboard found four wheels and my tennis shoes found the grip tape.

Planes and helicopters blinking red between the stars whispered sweet secrets of death. I kept my eyes on the concrete, leaning around a fire hydrant here, a signpost there, a homeless person over here. With my eyes like that, ready to slalom through the various obstacles on the sidewalk, I didn't see her stopped there at the corner until it was too late.

I hopped off the board and it kept rolling into the crosswalk. I bit through the donut in my mouth, and it fell to the ground. My shoes stutter-stepped and skidded but stayed underneath me, just barely. I still had to put a hand up to catch myself from slamming into her. Even that knocked her off balance and she almost fell into the street.

"Sorry! Sorry," I said, a little more composed the second time. "I wasn't watching. Didn't mean to… You spilled your coffee."

Eyes safer on her cup than meeting mine, she shrugged. "I really wasn't drinking it anyway. I should be in bed, asleep."

"We work together," I said. "I mean, I saw you in the office today."

Our eyes met, but only briefly. Hers were beautiful and glistening peaceful twinkles of light. She nodded. "I've seen you there too."

"Good teams, like, the best teams, they don't let new people in very easily," I said, mumbling over my words. "It's like special operations teams in the military. They have to test out the new guys. Make sure they're…"

Across the street, there was a food truck, all the windows shut and closed up, but the LED sign on top of the truck still flashed. As I rambled about small group dynamics, the flashes from the food truck spoke of other things.

TACOS - "We're coming for you."

GYROS - "We'll eat your brains straight through your ears."

SHAWARMA - "And lick your skull dry."

PIZZA BY THE SLICE - "And we are hungry."

"Do you see them?" the girl said.

From every security camera, electronic lock, transformer, and glowing window in the city. From every flashing light in a city full of millions. "See what?" I asked.

"They've been following me," she whispered. Her eyes were locked just over my shoulders. "Look."

I checked behind me. Shadows. Tiny pinpricks of white light flashing and pulsing. Over her shoulders, the demons in rotting black cloaks floated out of the reflections of the food truck's light. Bats flapped their holey wings between the stars. I crushed my eyelids shut.

"I'd rather not," I said.

"I gotta go," she said. "See you at work tomorrow."

She turned and ran off between the leering drooling demons with their shining eyes and elongated claws. They didn't seem to notice her. She slipped past them. Their cold blue eyes fixed on me. Feet hidden by moth-eaten black wool hovered their bodies closer and closer.

I turned the opposite way, abandoned my skateboard and the girl, and ran.

The girl I saw just before we collided back there on the street corner. The big guy in the all-black business suit? Not so much. His black tie hung untied around his tree-stump neck. The tails of his white shirt hung out of his belt. Gin breath plumed from his mouth like smoke from a tire fire. "Where's she running off to so quick?" he said.

From the shadows, his monochromatic cohorts stepped up to his flanks. The one on the right wore his tie still knotted but loose, six inches from his neck. The other's tie dangled like a black tongue out of the pocket of his suit coat. Mister Loose Tie pulled a swig of a tall and narrow glass bottle and passed it behind Hung Tied's back to No Tie.

99

My feet did the smartest things and let the rebound of crashing into Hung Tie carry me back away from them.

"I don't... Who?" I stalled till my brain could come up with something smarter to say.

"You know who," Loose Tie said.

"Hey, aren't you the kid from the mailroom?" No Tie said.

"You should be in bed, little boy," Hung Tie said.

"I... I was just going," I said and turned. It didn't take long before I was running as if I was a little kid racing home to mom. My skateboard was back this way anyway. They laughed to each other as their volume faded to nothing behind him. When I found my skateboard on its wheels in the middle of the crosswalk, I didn't bother to pick it up and carry it. Just hopped right on and started pushing.

Morning came with sharp sunlight and the growing drone of the city before I caught a second of sleep. I walked to the office in my suit. No skateboarding in those clothes. Along the way, I reminded myself that this was my decision to come here, to jump into the deep end, to go after this internship to begin with. I could have gone to the local community college like a lot of my friends. Could have stayed home. Could have stuck with the safe and familiar. Still could. A single word to my supervisor, and they'd let me go and take on the next kid eager for the opportunity.

Engineers and developers and salarymen and interns and clerks and programming geniuses pushed through the doors into the big atrium-like ocean waves coming into shore. The girl from last night was just a few heads over. I could tell by the look in her eyes, she didn't sleep any last night either. The tide washed us into different elevators.

The day rolled on like a truck careening down a hill without a driver. An assembly line of petty tasks that never ended. I almost fell asleep while making copies. The scanner bulb tracked with each copy, as audible as it was visible, and it only had one thing to say to me.

"Tonight."

"Tonight."

"Tonight."

"Tonight."

"Are you done with those yet? Hey you remembered to print it double-sided, right? Make sure they're correlated," a man said. In the basement of my mind, I registered that Hung Tie had tied his tie up in a smart Windsor, right up against his Adam's apple. Did he recognize me from last night? He pretended he didn't, so I pretended I didn't recognize him.

"When you're done with those, I need a hundred copies of these," he said. "Single-sided, stapled in the top right corner. Make sure the toner doesn't run out halfway through like last time. Got it?"

"Got it," I said.

"When you're done, bring them down to R and D," Hung Tie said. "And be quick about it."

On the last page of the report, there was a yellow sticky note covering some of the words. I peeled it off and stuck it to the edge of the printer so it wouldn't obscure the hundred copies I was about to make. Had to do a good job with these petty tasks if I wanted to stay on. Didn't matter if I was running on no sleep. Details like this mattered.

The copy machine continued to flash, "Tonight. Tonight. Tonight."

The sticky note read, "Animal testing complete. Move onto next phase."

Another long long night. I never bothered to change clothes or climb into bed. I sat on the couch in front of a dead TV deep into the night. At the bottom right of the frame, a little red LED blinked ever so dully. No words this time around. But the visuals… God damn the visuals. They grew out of that little red dot like it was a drop of blood in a pool that stained the water from edge to edge. And out of that pool of candy apple blood, came black twisting arms. Human arms, only as dark as charcoal and too long. They stretched out for me and when they couldn't reach any further, the bones snapped at ninety degrees and grew new elbows. Like photo-negative lightning bolts against a violent red sky.

I never thought of myself as a coward. Never really thought of myself as a brave hero either. I just wanted a good job and a steady paycheck. I thought this would be easy. Thought it would be fun. When I twisted away from my TV and buried my face in my knees and arms, the tears poured out of me. A distant part of me thought of myself as a little baby coward, wanting to run back home to mommy. But mostly, I didn't want those stretching arms to reach me.

What the hell was happening to me? Was it this place? These things? When exactly had I lost my mind?

Something sharp and as hard as steel dragged along my forearm, from wrist to elbow. Midway down, it flicked a finger and sliced the claw into my skin. Warm blood whipped down over my legs and onto the couch. The shock and the pain were enough to startle me out of my ball. I jumped off the end of the couch to make a run for the door but stopped.

The DI Companion sat between me and the door, visually humming from that round blue top, listening, waiting… I'd never spoken a word to that thing. Hadn't touched it yet. A gift from the company to all the interns. A prototype still in testing. Battery-powered, portable, and impossible to turn off. It emitted a lightning-blue halo onto the apartment's ceiling. With each surge and ebb the light drew hands and claws out of the ceiling. They stretched down like streams of rain pouring down into a cenote.

When I shut my eyes, I could still see them. After-images pressed against my eyelids. I breathed in deep, squatted like a sprinter in the blocks, then opened my eyes and bolted before I could change my mind. I snatched the DI Companion off the coffee table without breaking stride and crammed the soda-can-sized device into my back pocket so I'd have hands to grab my tennis shoes and my skateboard. Then I was out the door.

I wheezed against the exterior of my apartment door as if I'd run a marathon. That was okay. I had time to catch my breath now.

One end of the hallway was dark. A window looked out over the commuter train tracks. While I crammed my right foot into one shoe, the train came thundering by. Each window flashed by like the cell of cheap stop-motion animation. Each frame a still of a passenger. Each passenger another dead anonymous face, and a flash of light. Between each flicker, the shadows of the hallway shifted and moved and grew. Like cephalopods out of the aphotic deep, pale white writhing limbs wormed out of the darkness at the end of the hall, crawling towards me like creeper vines in time-lapse photography synced to the light of the passing train.

I bunny-hopped away from the window and the albino octopodol tentacles so I could shove my foot into my other shoes. I was still wearing my dress socks, black trousers, white button-up shirt, and black tie from work. Not ideal riding attire, but nothing about this was ideal. When the DI Companion tried to slip out of my butt pocket,

I crammed it back in, lighted-top down. By the time I reached the spasming fluorescent lights pouring spider-legs from its fixture, I was on my board and rolling fast and crouching low.

Outside, the streets were empty except for the multitude of tiny lights all around me. Left, right, up, down, they consumed me. The ones too dim or far away to show me horrors whispered into my ears. The lights near me grew fangs and claws and tentacles and expanded into pools of blood and viscera. Nothing I could do about that. Not yet. I dropped the skateboard onto the sidewalk and focused on that rhythmic clack clack clack of wheels against cracks.

All those things were still out there. It didn't matter if I wasn't looking. Like motor oil through a spaghetti strainer, they streamed out of every twinkle of light. Sludge and creatures. Bats and snakes and spiders and crustaceans. But also those demons in rotting black cloaks with jutting underbites and massive tusks.

Occasionally, I had to glance up. To check for traffic, street poles, and people. The nose of my skateboard swerved, and I leaned around them. But there was nothing I could do about the demons. It didn't seem to matter how fast I rode. They were always behind me, always closing in around me, always in front of me. They converged on me, shuffling their circle in like the closing teeth of a massive leviathan.

Smoke wafted off their shoulders and steam rose from the cool puddles where they stepped. Talons grew out of their fingertips, some so long they scraped the ground as they walked. Others were just as long, but stretched out towards me, coming closer to me every moment.

I kicked off the sidewalk, focused on that clank clank clank of the sidewalk, and tried to quicken the tempo. Ahead, beyond the zit zit zit flashes of a broken streetlight and the lumbering horde of demons, there was a warm orange glow. I put my head down and pushed hard off the concrete. The deck descended down a ramp off the curb, over the crosswalk, and back up the rise of the next sidewalk. From there, I felt the heat of that orange light as much as saw it. It was steady, consistent, inviting, and I knew where it led.

The tail of my board skidded across the cement as I manualled to a stop before the donut shop. It was quiet for a moment, as I looked through the glass and saw who I almost knew I'd find there: the girl, and Hung Tie, Loose Tie, and No Tie all moving in around her. How did I know she'd be here? How did they know? They hadn't reached her yet. Must have come to the donut shop not long before me. But they closed in around her like the demons closing in around me.

From the top down, the entire building bled black ooze. Monsters with teeth and spines and multitudes of legs gathered around. The demons didn't rush in now that I was stopped. They hung just outside of fingernail reach.

"Agony, for you and for her," a demon breathed out behind me.

"Sorrow."

"Mystery."

"Death, boy," the chorus of them whispered.

What better reason to go in and get a donut?

The jingle bells clunked, toneless and joyless against the glass. Between their black suits, the girl's eyes contacted mine. The big guys didn't turn to look. They just moved in closer. No Tie pulled his tie out of his collar and off his neck and crammed it in a pocket. Loose tie tipped back a bottle of gin.

"You didn't want to come out with us earlier tonight?" Hung Tie asked the girl. "You know, we can tell when you leave your apartment. Why didn't you come out? Why'd you only come out now? Don't you like us?"

Hell behind me. Hell before me. Why had I come here? Why had I ever left home?

"'Scuse me?" I managed to say over the screeches of long fingernails against the windows.

Loose Tie was the only one of the three who even bothered to turn and see me. He waved me away with the hand still holding the gin bottle. "Piss off, kid."

"You should come with us," Hung Tie said to the girl. "We just want to show you a good time. We're not bad guys."

"Hey," I said a little louder, louder than all those claws on every pane around the fishbowl donut shop. "Excuse me."

No Tie yelled over his shoulder, "Order your donut and get the hell out of here already."

"Bavarian creme with black coffee, right?" the man behind the counter said. "I'll get it and then you can get out."

Hung Tie only stepped closer to the girl, over her as she sat by herself at a table.

104

"No coffee," I said. "No donuts. But I have something for all of you."

My words must have been loud enough to drown out the sound of the demons trying to dig their way into the shop, or maybe that sound finally got their attention. Hung Tie, Loose Tie, and No Tie turned around, squaring up to me, feet planted wide apart. Hung Tie cracked his knuckles. No Tie laughed. Loose Tie raised up the gin bottle so he could hold it and point at me with the same hand.

Before he could tell me how badly they were going to kick my ass, I slipped the DI Companion from my back pocket and let it roll over the cracked linoleum.

It flashed like a strobe, as brilliant and violent as white phosphorus, only blue. So bright that between flashes, the donut store seemed pitch black. And out of the blackness, the demons strode with their tusks bared and their impossibly long fingernails reaching out. Serpents and arachnids and arthropods and cephalopods came out of the darkness with them. So did the words and whispers.

"Kill, kill, kill."

"Blood. Thirsty for blood."

"Murder."

The monochromatic trio of men locked eyes on the DI Companion. Their bodies tried to push back and turn and move away, but their eyes were fixed on the flashing blue puck as if tethered by ropes and harpoons. All around them, the demons and hellions closed in.

Through it all, I almost missed the girl bolting for the side door.

As I followed her, my ears rang and bled from the volume of the screams.

The city was quietest just before dawn. No traffic. No sirens. The trains were far away and far between. No planes in the sky. A pause in an otherwise constant cacophony. She heard me coming, not rattling down the sidewalk on my skateboard, but shuffling along in my tennis shoes. I held the board in my right hand and came up along her left side.

"Hey," I said. "You okay?"

She just nodded.

We walked in silence for half a block.

"The lights… they're quiet out here," she said. "Not like back in my apartment. In there… I can't sleep."

105

I nodded.

"Does that sound crazy to you?" she asked me.

"No," I said. "And I think I can fix it. If you want."

She nodded.

It was only another hour or so until work started. Not enough time for sleep, but enough to find some peace. As the crowds piled into the atrium and towards the elevators, I caught her eyes again. This time, she caught mine too, and when she did, she smiled.

Instant War

First published in Bullet Points, Vol 4, Issue 1 in January 2024

There were balloons. Presents. Cake. Ice cream. Little screaming banshees everywhere I tried to step. Then there was me, dressed in jeans, a T-shirt and flip-flops. A bad shave. A thousand-meter stare. Tinnitus playing in my ears. Drunk before noon at a little kid's birthday party. I stood out like a dildo in the middle of a menorah. What the hell was I doing here?

I should be forty light years away, fighting a war I had no stakes in, dying next to my brothers, or at least surviving next to them as they died. I didn't want to be there, but I couldn't help but need to be on Diaterous 74.

A pack of little kids sprinted past me. I stood there in the kitchen and chugged my beer.

There's an old saying that goes, "Amateurs study tactics. Professionals study logistics." So, I guess as soon as we mastered teleportation, and there was no longer a need to study logistics, we all became amateurs. I felt like an amateur, standing there trying to be a normal human being with my wife, Lisa, at a party at her second-cousin-or-something-or-other's house. I tried to be social. Tried to be polite. Tried to pretend like we weren't at war. Tried not to think about the next Pick-Up. Tried not to think about tactics and death. Tried to be a civilian like everybody else.

It wasn't working.

"How goes the battle?" her uncle said. I think it was her uncle. Maybe a cousin. The birthday boy's dad. An in-law for all of the six months Lisa and I had been married. How much of that time was I even around for?

"What?" I said.

"How you doing there, Mitch my boy?" Uncle Who-Gives-a-Shit rephrased.

So, not like a SITREP from the frontlines then? Not really interested in our forward progress across the Diaterian hellscape forty light years from here. Not actually concerned with our casualty/kill ratio. Couldn't give a shit if Johansen and the guys were still alive in that muddy crater I left them in. Nope. Not this guy. This jack-wagon was completely oblivious to the fact that I was anticipating the next Pick-Up like a sprinter in the blocks.

"I'm good," I said, clutching my beer, my only respite in this particular hell.

"Well, I sure as hell hope those jackasses in office can pull their heads out of their asses and bring you boys home for good one of these days," Cousin Go-Fuck-Yourself said.

Yeah. Politics. Let's talk fucking politics. I took another drink, knowing they'd evaporate the alcohol from my blood the instant they brought me back to the Staging Area. Might as well drink up while I could. The beer felt good going down. Although, I was pretty sure it would have felt better smashed against Uncle Fuckface's big round melon.

I nodded. Said, "Yup," because it was the safe answer. Because if I said little to him, he'd have little to say back.

He started up again, talking about what some politician said on some news stream about peace talks and conciliations.

That was enough of that. So, I looked him straight in his stupid face and said, "I can't fucking stand it in here. I gotta go." That was me being polite.

I drained the rest of the beer, turned to the front of the house, and spotted my wife. On the way out I hooked an arm around Lisa and dragged her with me through the front door.

"Mitch… Mitch, what the hell!" she swore at me as soon as we were outside.

I stopped pulling on her and she stopped there on the stoop. I went out into the yard. We were in farm country. Deep in the Midwest. Not a mountain or a hill or a building from horizon to horizon. The ground was hard-packed black dirt. The driveway was gravel.

"I can't do it. I can't take one more second in there, Lisa," I said.

"Really, Mitch? Do we really have to fight about this? It's a kid's birthday party. A birthday party," she said.

"Lisa…" She had a point. After all, who can't hack a damn birthday party? But right then? I should have been on Diaterous 74. "Can we just go?" I asked.

She stood just outside the front door, one hand on a hip, mouth a little agape in disbelief. Yeah. We weren't going anywhere. "You know, Mitch, the world doesn't stop turning every time they zap you back home. You have no idea how hard this is for me."

"How hard it is for you?" Sure. A full-blown fight at a kid's birthday party. Why the hell not? "How hard for you? Are you even listening to yourself?"

"Yes, Mitch. Hard for me. Every time you show up, I drop everything and try to do whatever I can to keep us together. To keep our marriage together. And every time I feel like we're making a centimeter of progress-"

109

I didn't hear the rest of her sentence. Didn't get to see her spit her words at me. Didn't get to see her storm off. Sure as shit didn't get to say goodbye. No kiss. No hug. No make-up sex. One moment I was in Uncle Shit-For-Brain's front yard. The next I was in the Staging Area, a station halfway between Earth and Diaterous 74 and the war. I guess that's one way to win an argument.

"Welcome back, Gunny," the lab tech said. "Sober?"

I checked myself for a second. "Like a stone," I said. "Talk about a buzzkill."

I was naked and cold. I brought nothing with me from the farmhouse and would bring nothing back. Just me, and the transponder they used to locate me embedded into the flesh in my wrist. It pulsed a red and subtle light.

The memory of Lisa standing on the farmhouse's front stoop, resilient, eyes on fire... That stuck with me. I loved her angry. I loved her when she was sweet too, but something about her tenacity intoxicated me. My body was in outer space, but my mind lingered there in the farmyard. The more I tried to remember, the more the image faded away. My head swam.

It always took me a few seconds to re-orientate myself after Pick-Up. I looked around the Staging Area room. The walls were glistening metal. Floor and ceiling were metal. The only thing that wasn't steel were all the monitors and screens and one small window that looked out of the station into the eternity of space. We were a billion miles from any other outpost.

"Any injuries? Illnesses? Abnormalities?" the tech said. I didn't know why he bothered asking me. He was busy checking the scanners and read-outs on his tablet that told him more information about me than I could ever provide.

"Abnormalities? Yeah. This whole fucking circus."

"Biology is a Go. Step forward for uniform and armament," the tech said.

I did. There were boot prints painted on the floor. I put my bare feet on the yellow paint, careful to keep all my little toes inside the foot shape. They told stories at Boot about a guy with a bigger-than average wang. When the suit clamped on him, they say half his dick didn't make it inside the suit and fell to the floor, right between those two yellow-paint footprints. A ridiculous story told by stupid privates. Still, I closed my eyes, held my breath, and tried to retract my scrotum.

The suit came over me like a bear trap. Two halves, front and back, came out of the walls and snapped me inside. All of me, thank God. The exo-armor encased me from head to toe. Life-support systems. Comms equipment. Pneumatic-assisted limbs. Thrusters for zero-gee navigation.

"Uniform diagnostics are a Go," the tech said. His voice came through my helmet now. He picked a combat blaster out of a weapons closet and handed it to me. "Your armament, gunny. Your uniform is fully stocked. Combat knife. Six frags. Six flashbangs. Seven magazines."

I performed a functions check on the rifle by muscle memory, as automatic as cracking off a bottle top when handed a beer. The weapon was clean. The action rode smooth. I took an ammo magazine magnetized to my chest and got ready to slam it into the bottom of the blaster.

Another voice came over my comms. "Gunnery Sergeant Andrews?"

"Send it," I said.

"Captain Mathews here. Sorry for pulling your leave short. We're surging against the enemy. Need all boots-on-ground. You'll be joining Angel Platoon, a base-of-fire element a hundred yards to the enemy front. You'll lead Fire Team Two One. We'll be dropping in a flank element as soon as your platoon establishes contact. This will be Battle Drill Number One, by-the-book."

"Understood, sir," I said. My fingers played with the magazine.

The lab tech came into the view of my visor. He ushered me back into the teleporter. "Step back for Drop-Off. Lock and load, gunny."

"And roger," I said, slapped the magazine into the bottom of the weapon, and charged the action. My heart thumped. Skin grew goose-pimples. Way too much sweat. If someone can stand in the teleporter, ready for Drop-Off, and not feel something… man, they're not human. "Locked and loaded."

The captain was back in my ear. "The enemy's dug in deep and heavily armed. We need every barrel on target. Drop-Off in five. Any questions, gunny?"

"Suppose it's too late to go back to the birthday party?"

They fucked up the Drop-Off. Guys were coming in one by one when we should have arrived simultaneously. The first sorry fucker to drop, I guess he was the corpse at my feet. He blew our element of surprise. Then the Diaterians blew a decimeter-wide hole through his chest. When the salvo of laser fire burnt the thin atmosphere around me, I dropped just as flat as he was.

Diaterous was mostly mud and water. I never saw any plants or wild animals here. Mud. Dirt. The occasional enemy steel bunker. Lots of dead bodies. Headquarters didn't bother zapping back the corpses. I guess that was too much like logistics for their tastes. A dark purple sky like a giant bruise hung overhead, day or night. Your standard battlefield scene.

I couldn't see much from where I lay. By now everyone was belly to the ground, either because they were dead or didn't want to be dead. I did a quick headcount of my Fire Team. Johansen, Miller, and Everette were alive and present for duty.

"Angel Six here," a voice came over the comms in my helmet. That'd be the lieutenant. I wondered which college simulator they pulled this kid out of. "Orientate your fire to one four one and acquire the target. We need to establish the base of fire–"

His voice cut off. I glanced down below my visor to all the digital read-outs and saw that the LT just bought it. Well, this was going fan-fucking-tastic.

"Angel Seven, here. Follow my lead." The Platoon Sergeant: somebody with some drop experience. "Stay low. Move slow to the crest of this trench. Suppressive fire. We got the ammo. We just have to put it on target. Go."

He was right. If we didn't heat up the objective, the flanking element would be left with their asses hanging in the breeze. Time to get to work. I switched over to my fire team comms net.

"Alright boys, nice and slow. Up the trench," I told them, all while Diaterian laser bolts raked overhead.

As I started crawling up the shallow slope, I saw my guys moving on either side of me. That was good. Some semblance of order. With the pneumatic-assisted suit, it didn't take long to crest the slew and spot the target. One of those featureless steel bunkers that scattered this hell hole.

"Target acquired," Johansen said.

"Engage," I ordered.

Our lasers lit up the ever-night. Accurate Diaterian laser-fire responded. It hammered around us and vaporized the wet right out of the mud. Made us wish we could push deeper into the reddish slop that was the topsoil. Then, the laser fire stopped.

"Lay it on 'em!" I yelled. If they didn't want to fight, we'd show them that we did. But why would they stop firing? Why would we?

113

"Flankers!" Angel Seven yelled over the platoon net. "On our nine. Spread out. First squad, move-"

Another light went out below my visor. So much for Angel Seven.

I saw the Diaterians charging our left flank. They were coming quick. Bundles of metallic prehensile limbs that scrambled towards us like giant spiders. Laser fire pumped out from their thoracic centers.

They had us in an enfilade in that slew, all lined up in a row. More laser fire seared mud and atmosphere and bodies. Comms were chaos. Guys were dropping like flies. Why wasn't First Squad Leader taking charge of this shitshow? Where were our flankers?

I flicked a switch in my glove and changed comms nets. "Base, this is Angel Two One, requesting immediate extraction. Call off the assault. We do not have fire superiority. Repeat, we do not-"

And like a snap of a magician's fingers, I was back in Cousin Chicken-fucker's front yard, as naked as the day I was born. I crumpled down into the gravel driveway. The bright sunlight blinded my eyes. The hard-packed gravel hurt against my bare skin. This place was Diaterous' mirror opposite.

My body shook. Funny thing how adrenaline works. Cool as a cucumber in the moment, but after? My own little personal earthquake rattled away from inside my chest.

They pulled us out and plopped us right back where they found us. It was Standard Operating Procedure. Saves on overhead. Eliminates the logistical demand for garrisons and billets and chow and all that. Lets them focus on tactics. Allows us to be amateurs.

I wonder how many died before they zapped us out of that clusterfuck. And how soon till they dropped us back into it?

The party was still going on inside. Were they singing Happy Birthday? Did I miss them cutting the cake? Were they unwrapping presents? Like I gave a fuck.

I got up because if I didn't soon, they'd zap some cops here to arrest me for exposing myself to minors. There were clothes in my car. I'd gotten used to suddenly finding myself naked. I had to wonder though, what happened to my old clothes? What happened to my armor I was wearing when they zapped me here?

I climbed into the back seat of the car me and Lisa came in. Hard to call it a car really. No tires. No gas, brake, or steering wheel. Just four doors and four seats. A computer with some buttons on the front dash that ran the teleportation. There was a duffel bag with my usual jeans, a cheap T-shirt, and flip-flops inside. I got dressed and leaned back.

Where the hell was Lisa? What would she say to me this time? What was I supposed to do now? Go back into the party and try to build up my buzz again? I fixated on the "Travel" button built into the center of the dash. The coordinates for our apartment were already programmed into the computer. All I had to do was hit a button and I could ditch this debacle.

Fuck me.

I got out of the car.

Lisa and I got married six months ago. I figured out of those six months we'd spent about three of those months together. But we'd known each other for a lot longer than that. Years. Years uninterrupted by combat. Sane years.

We'd actually been to this particular uncle's/cousin's house before. I decided then that I should learn if he was her cousin or her uncle. It wasn't like he was both. They

115

weren't that redneck. I just never bothered to remember. All those little details seemed infinitely unimportant when you're zapped out of a no-shit-people-dying combat zone.

Point was, we'd been here before. Hid from the crowd here before. We'd been through all this shit before. Together.

I walked around the house to the backyard. She was right where I thought she'd be, sitting on an old rusty swing set. Decades of toddler shoes had swept deep gouges out of the lawn underneath each seat. Lisa sat on one of those seats, chin in her chest, long blonde hair hanging over her face, fingers clawed into her scalp.

My flip-flops flipped and flopped as I came around the house. She looked up as soon as she heard them, knowing it was me. What other jackass wears dollar-store flip-flops wherever he went?

Her face was flush. Eyes red. Cheeks wet. It took her a millisecond to leave the swing. She ran. I trotted to her in my stupid footwear, my nerves still shaking, sweat already soaking through my new t-shirt. She hugged me, but if she wasn't fifty pounds lighter than me it would have been a full-blown linebacker tackle. I wrapped her up and she buried her face in my shoulder.

"I'm sorry. I'm sorry. I'm so sorry…" she was saying.

This didn't feel like winning an argument.

"It's okay. I'm okay. We're alright," I said. "I'm sorry. I was a dick."

She was shaking too now. Her breaths were shallow. Heart racing. A legit panic attack. She'd just had me snatched away from her, maybe to die and never come back again, our last moments together spent yelling at each other. I knew it wouldn't hurt her so much if she didn't love me just as fiercely. It broke her.

I knew this was one of those moments when I was supposed to console her. Comfort her. But how the hell was I supposed to turn on a dime like that? A cold-hearted killer one second, a caring counselor the next?

"I can't do this," she managed. "You can't leave me like that."

"I…" What? I'd what? I wouldn't? I'd promise to change? I'd make it up to her? What?

"This has got to stop, Mitch. It's killing me."

There was no lie or exaggeration in her. This was her, defenses down, telling me what was what. I didn't have a thing to say back to her. I just held her as close as I could.

Then she was gone from my arms. I was back at the Staging Area. Metal walls. Video monitors. Armament. The jerk-off lab tech and me, a million miles from the rest of reality.

"Sober?" the lab tech asked.

"You gotta be shitting me," I said.

"Biology is a Go. Step forward for uniform and armament."

"You gotta be fist-fucking me? Are you fist-fucking me?"

"Gunny," the lab tech said. "Step forward for uniform and armament."

"I just left… I just fucking left twice now! Where are my fucking clothes?" I said. "I mean it. I wanna know where my goddamn clothes are. This shit's getting expensive."

"Gunny?" the captain's voice filled the small room. A monitor flickered and his old ragged face appeared. "Gunny, there's no time. We are outnumbered and on the verge of losing critical terrain. We need to hold this ground if we're going to maintain a beachhead on Diaterious 74. Suit up and get in the fight. Now."

117

I looked down at the pulsing red light sewn into my wrist. Enough of it protruded from my skin to get a good firm grip of it. "So help me, you zap me one more time…" I stepped forward and put both of my bare feet back in the yellow prints on the floor.

I sucked in my diaphragm and pulled up on my nuts as much as I could. Then I ripped that fucking transponder out of my wrist and let it drop to the floor like the tip of a well-endowed cock. It bounced outside of those yellow footprints. Their leash around my neck was gone. Blood from my wrist fell like rain on the steel deck. The suit was on me a blink later.

"Uniform diagnostics are a Go," the tech said and handed me my rifle. "You have a full inventory. Step back for Drop-Off. Quickly, please."

"Gunny, your call sign will be Angel Seven. We're out of lieutenants so you'll have the platoon," the captain was telling me. I heard his words, but in my head, Lisa's pleas absorbed my attention.

This has to stop. It's killing me.

"Your platoon will be the flanking element. We've established a base of fire, but it won't hold long."

"You're not pulling me out of there. And don't you go pulling any of my platoon out either. This time we're staying till the job's done," I said.

"Drop in five seconds."

"This has to stop."

Saints of Skid Row

First published in Typewriters and Whiskey in 2024

Come in from the cold my brothers and sisters. Welcome. Welcome to the House of God, you who are weak and heavy laden. I beseech thee, come and sit. For the Lord said "Bring the homeless, the jobless, the addicted, the rejected and exiled unto me." And so today, he will heal all of us modern day lepers. We've been cast aside from the world's feasts, so come to mine. We'll make our own table and upon it set the most satisfying meal. Listen to me, my scabs and scrubs and droogs, and I will tell you how we came to this place. I am not the beginning nor the end, but I was here when it first started.

A young girl was standing where I am now, at the front of this abandoned basement of an animal shelter. The light was dim. The air was hot and thick from the smoldering fires. Smoke crept from the open mouths of the furnaces then just as it does now. There were rows and rows of rusted and bent folding chairs, salvaged from the trash, just like those who would occupy them. This pulpit was up here at the front, exactly where it stands now. The altar, just a cardboard box standing upside down on its open top, just as I'd found it that day. And upon it stood this child's pretty pink plastic tea set. Tiny cups and saucers and a pot with flowers printed on its belly were ready for the service. She, Dorothea, our messiah, stood behind this pulpit on a milk crate so she had to step up before seeing over the edge. This place looked nothing like the holy grounds it is. Even now, it doesn't look like a sacred place to the uninitiated. I was at the back entrance, not yet with enough courage to come before her, to join the feast, to sup and receive her grace. But I watched from the back.

I will be honest with you, my fellow nameless, placeless, unseen, sick, and insane wandering hordes. I didn't believe my eyes when I first came here. Dorothea was such a diminutive and feral thing. What I walked into, it should have been a nice little tea party, her at a small table surrounded by her stuffed animals, pouring tea for her guests. And I wanted to be that loving father who wouldn't be too manly to sit with his daughter and put on a big sunhat and sip water from a plastic cup to make her happy. I would have killed for that opportunity to provide her that comfort. But we do things differently in this community. She had much larger ambitions in mind. But just like a father, I was drawn in by her glamour. By the pouring of the magic tea.

She was dressed in her Sunday finest: a billowing dress, lightly colored, flowers printed on the fine material, lace bloomed from the collar and wrists. Just like her, the dress had once been pristine but was now marred with the filth of the streets. And she had brought animals to her meal as well. Some of them are still here tonight. Dressed in equal elegance, she'd brought them here and set them up in the chairs. How lucky they are, to be found by her, hauled out and brought back from the dead, and set in this place of worship, and able to receive her redemption.

This was a kill shelter, before it was shut down. The worst kind of animal shelter in the nastiest part of this putrid city. A shelter most unworthy of its name. A place that understood nothing of redemption and renewal. A place that specialized in discarding the unwanted. But lo! She set a table in the house of our enemies. It was clear from the start that this poor homeless girl, no parents or siblings to comfort her, saw the uncremated dead left behind when the doors closed as her very own collection of stuffed animals. As her friends. She must have been so lonely, so desperate for companionship, that when she found them in the freezers, waiting for all eternity for their turn in the kiln, she pulled them out and placed them in the chairs they're in today. Look upon our honored guests. Her first converts sit among us, donned in gay attire, in dresses and suit jackets, with hats and bows, just as she prepared them.

I admit it. When I first came through that door and saw her standing here behind this podium and saw them seated in front of her as her attentive congregation, I was dismayed. I recognized them immediately for what they were: house pets put to sleep by their previous owners. Cats and dogs mostly. A boa constrictor here in the second row. An iguana in an aisle seat. I'm not sure if you can see them, but there is a queue of passed-on guinea pigs and hamsters between the altar and the front row, lined up like soldiers on guard duty. All of their eyes are fogged over. Their hair or scales are still wet with frost. No doubt you've discovered their smell. Perhaps they had gotten too old and were no longer house-trained. Or maybe they bit. Or maybe they were just unloved. She found them. And with them, this parish of misfits, she filled the hole in her soul.

When my heart reached that epiphany, that this was not a thing morbid or macabre, I was no longer shocked by the sight or the smell or the taste of the smoke rolling from the furnaces. This was a thing of pure unadulterated beauty. No, my fellow panhandlers and pimps and perverts, I was not repulsed. I was enamored. I was enraptured. And then she called me up from the back of this room, to her altar.

"Come on," she called in that sing-song voice only little girls can have. "I see you back there. You're not hiding very well. Come have some tea with me."

And so, I shuffled past the roadkill calico, the dead-eyed dachshund, the frozen boa constrictor halfway through shredding its last skin. I avoided eye contact with the

121

painted turtle peeking from his shell. I pretended not to smell the black lab wearing the pink and blue sundress. I ignored the black soot around each of their mouths.

There were no chairs in front of this cardboard box altar and its tea set, so I knelt as any supplicant should. The glass of my bottle of booze clinked down against the concrete. Then she poured from the tea pot into my cup, the stream black and dusty. Tiny granules, not fluid, filled my cup to the brim. She tapped the spout against the rim of my cup and a few more grains of ash fell in.

"What is it?" I asked her.

"It will make you feel better. It's like medicine," she told me.

Ashes. I could tell that much before putting the cup to my lips. And it was clear where she'd gotten them from. But I didn't yet know if she understood what the ashes were before entering the kiln.

"Where are your parents? Don't you have a brother or sister who could—"

She twisted her head no, meaning she had none, or perhaps meaning she didn't want to talk about the subject.

"I used to have a family," I confessed. In order to receive the sacrament, one must be in a state of grace. "Not anymore. I don't have anyone anymore."

They say the cops, when they want you to keep going on and confessing more than you should, won't respond and will just let you fill the void of silence with more things you shouldn't say. In the same manner, she said nothing.

"When I got in my accident, I didn't even remember getting behind the wheel. Why my wife didn't stop me, why my kids didn't kick and scream until I realized the shape I was in, I don't know. Or maybe they did fuss and fight, and I was just too drunk to listen. I don't know. But I got behind the wheel, and they rode with me." I poured my broken soul out to this girl. And she listened more attentively than any therapist or judge

122

or jury. And she understood. Because of course she would. It was clear she'd been through something similar, this pretty young thing, she had pains and losses as well. "That one irrevocable decision... That one mistake... It cost me everything. My family. My car. My license. My job. My house. My life... all from that one choice."

"Everybody makes mistakes," Dorothea told me. And then, with that enigmatic smile of hers, "Drink it! You'll like it, I promise."

"But... It's from one of them, isn't it?" I asked her, gesturing to the animals in the old folding chairs behind me. Not because I didn't know, but to see if she knew. If she understood what she was asking of me.

"There's no food here, so we have to feed each other," she said simply. Dorothea had such a simple way of stating the complex.

That was her wisdom. Clear, concise, and almost clairvoyant. Of course, she knew where the ashes came from. See, when they shut down the shelter, it was done so quickly it was as if the workers had been taken up by the Rapture. Paperwork dropped to the floor by hands taken into heaven. Chairs not even pushed back from their desks before being vacated. Legal pads only half full of notes. Animals waiting in cages to be adopted or killed until they starved to death. The once beloved pets spared from the torture of starvation sat in freezers waiting for the sweet release of the flames. The ones who'd made it into the fire still remained in the bottom of the ovens as unremoved ashes. Dorothea found those forgotten souls too. And as was her way, she brought them before us.

"You could feed them too, you know," she said, and I immediately comprehended the dual meaning of her words.

She understood the cyclic nature of the world, how we feed off others until it becomes our turn to be the feed. It was the fate of all the congregation. Of her. And eventually of me.

Fear found its way from those pleasant eyes into my heart. I'm ashamed of it, my fellow vagrants and tramps. She intimidated me with her steady, easy, gaze. But Dorothea also steeled my spirit and nailed my courage to the sticking place, as they say. I knew what I had to do, if I was to carry on.

I tipped back my cup. I coughed. A haze of carbonized house pets floated in the air. Dorothea laughed. Nothing could ever be as dry and hard to swallow as that first communion. But as I tried again and managed to move the first swallow down my throat, she put a finger under the teacup, urging me to go on. So I took. And I supped. And I gave thanks. For she had filled the empty part of me. A man's stomach can only be filled for a day, but as for his soul… My cup runneth over!

So, come to me, you sick, you lame, you speed freaks, you living dead. All of you derelicts and degenerates. You lost and broken souls, come unto me and I shall get you your fix. Commune with me, oh ye saints of skid row. Where is Dorothea, you ask? I assure you, she's here with her pretty pink tea set. Come and partake with me. Devour her purity of essence, her spirit, her wholesome, untainted soul. She will fill the voids inside of you, just like she filled in the things missing from me. She made me whole again, and she'll make you whole again as well.

Take eat. This is her body. Take drink. This is her blood.

Frequency Harmonics

First published on May 1st, 2023, in The Storyville Project, Book 3

The door creaked open with the lightest shove of my palm. Unlocked. Barely latched. Hardly what you'd call breaking and entering. Me and my imaginary dead sister stepped into the shadows.

One of these days Mary, all this is going to catch up with you.

"Not right now, sis. I respect you, and you know I love you, but for now, stay out of my fucking head," I whispered to her as I pulled out my phone and flipped through the screens.

The property was a rented-out pole barn made out of corrugated steel walls and big rolling garage doors currently shut and blocking out the morning sun. And thank God for that. The morning's eye-level glare stabbed my brain where I kept my hangovers. The inside of the building was divided up with sheetrock walls that didn't go all the way up to the ceiling. Exposed trusses and more corrugated steel for a roof. Bare concrete under my boots. There were lights and power, but I was trying to keep my profile low, so the lights stayed off and I relied on my phone's trusty flashlight app.

125

The light bounced off the unpainted, undecorated sheet rock until I found my way past a bathroom, a broom closet, and an office to the main work area. This part of the building, a thirty-by-thirty-foot space, was all workbenches, industrial shelving, and stacks of parts and cabling. Nobody home. Just me and my dead sister.

I never really knew her. Mom and dad never gave her a name. She died in the womb. We spent six months side-by-side, alive. Three more months with me just chilling in utero with her corpse. Miscarriages are common with twins. In our case, I got more than my fair share of the nutrients from the placenta. My sis starved while I got fat eating for two. A minor biological defect. It happens. I thought about that often, how close she was to being alive. How close I was to being a different person.

I'd like to think that if she'd lived, she would have lived a better life than I have. Been everything mom and dad wanted out of a daughter. Been the daughter they wanted instead of me. So that's how I made her out to be inside my head, a little goody two-shoes guardian angel on my shoulder who reminded me to cut back on drinking and maybe give up the cigarettes. Minor fictions that were truths in some other reality.

"Where the fuck did he go?" I said to an empty shop, my voice echoing off the metal walls.

He skipped bail on murder charges. Did you really expect him to show up to work on Monday? Why do you care anyway? You're wasting your life defending these people, Mary. I don't know why you do it, my nameless unborn sister said.

"This one's different. He doesn't feel like a murderer. Feels more like a family member than a criminal. Besides, somebody's got to stand up for us lower life forms."

Realizing there was no one to hide from, I found the big industrial light switch next to the garage door. Sodium-vapor lights popped, cracked, slowly warmed, and shed

126

a dim light over the room. I pulled out a pack of smokes and shot one out of the paper wrapper.

You know, I never received the gift of life like you. Least you could do is not squander the one you have by inhaling death in front of me.

"What are you gonna do? Get second-hand cancer and die twice?" I mumbled, the yet-unlit smoke bouncing between my lips.

A year ago, my client was working as an engineer for a military contractor designing radios full of cutting-edge digital encryptions and top-secret security protocols. Since then, he wigged out and rented this place in a rust-belt industrial park. Spent the last twelve months of his life complaining about headaches and obsessing over "frequency harmonics."

Before I was a public defender, I was a sheriff's deputy. In my department, I was the radio "smart girl." Nobody else had any interest in the extra duty, so I dabbled around and figured out how to configure our UHF network so we could talk through the county. That part of me, the radio-nerd part of me, understood my client's obsession. It was engrossing, how simple yet adaptable the technology was. Most people didn't get it. Figured radios were deader than disco now that we had podcasts, TikTok, and Disney+. The truth was, it all still came to us through radio frequencies. Cell signals, Wi-Fi, satellite TV… really no different than an old man playing with a HAM radio in the garage. Just different bandwidths on the spectrum.

As the bulbs overhead warmed, I washed over the workbenches covered in parts with the light from my phone. Transmitters, receivers, multimeters, soldering irons, amplifiers, broken hand mics… I kind of wanted to pull up a stool and play around with it all, but I was here on business. Tinkering with electronics was for another day.

I lit my cigarette.

So what were you hoping to find?

"Something. Anything. A clue as to why my client, a professional in his field, and a leader in his industry, would give it all up. He spent a year farting around disassembling and reassembling radios before murdering some bureaucrat from the FCC who happened to stop by his little shop here," I told my dead sister. "He's innocent, and something in this place will prove I'm right. The secret is hidden in his research. What did he have to hide? What was he looking to find?"

The FCC regulator came here on complaints of unregistered broadcasts. Pirate radio, essentially. Only my client wasn't blasting out censored rock n' roll or secret messages from a World War II numbers station. He was emitting squelch breaks and thousand-cycle tones. But what the hell for? And when the federal stooge came by, why not turn down the wattage instead of brain him to death with a lithium-ion battery?

Of all the equipment on the workbenches, only one set-up seemed to be operational. Nested amongst busted breadboards and cables with stripped pigtails was a multiband transmitter and a spectrum analyzer. The analyzer was on, and its green-hued screen showed a squiggly line at the bottom of a digital grid. The line on the graph represented all the atmospheric background noise. Static. Cosmic radiation. That was something people didn't understand with their worries about brain cancer from cell phones and microwaves and 5G. Radio waves were everywhere. It radiated from towers and satellites, light bulbs and TV screens, from solar flares and black holes a million light years away... There was no place on Earth where the spectrum didn't hum and dance. To me, it was the song of the universe. It touched everything. Came from everything. And to people like my client, it *was* everything.

I flipped on the multiband transmitter, saw it was tuned to thirty-five megahertz, a band of the spectrum owned by the military, and keyed the mic. Squelch broke, and I broadcasted the ambient noise of the workshop. The speaker crackled. The green line in the graph spiked between the numbers thirty and forty. Like ripples in still water, smaller spikes rose up around the numbers 70, 105, 140, 175, and barely rising about the static, the last molehill poked up around 210 megahertz. Multiples of the target frequency rippling up and down the spectrum.

"Harmonics," I pointed at the smaller and smaller spikes on the screen. "That's what he was getting after. Something about those repeating signals. Clones of the original, repeated forever until they faded into the background noise."

You know, they used to be proud of you, my sister said. *Back when you were a cop. When you were going through law school. When you passed the bar. Then you took a job as a public defender, working to set free the criminals you used to arrest. Now, when people ask mom and dad what you do, they lie.*

I ignored her and watched the amplitude dance up and down at thirty-five megahertz. It shot up and then shrank, and when it shrunk, the harmonic at seventy megahertz spiked.

"That's weird."

Your life choices. That's what's weird. You had infinite potential while I had none.

"The harmonics should shrink with the target frequency. They're echoes of the target frequency. Why…?"

The two spikes were oscillating now. When thirty-five shrank, seventy shot up. When one hundred and five rose, two ten shrank. And with the oscillations, the workshop seemed to fade in and out around me. Not the workshop. Maybe just those still-growing-brighter sodium arc lights. Maybe just my eyelids. My consciousness. Was I fainting? Blacking out? Usually, it took a whole hell of a lot more than a little whiskey in my

129

morning coffee before I passed out in a strange place. I fixated on the spectrum analyzer. My vision narrowed to a mile-long train tunnel, that dancing green line of spikes and harmonics the only visible thing in the universe.

As the tunnel closed around me, a single thought slipped through. Those harmonics, mimicking each other in parallel existences isolated and evenly spaced apart, never able to come in contact, never able to hear or affect the next harmonic over… I think I could relate.

Then…

"Where the fuck am I?" I mumbled with numb lips. Through groggy eyes, I saw a nice clean kitchen with granite countertops and brushed chrome appliances in a respectable split-entry single-family home.

From behind my back, a raspy masculine voice told me, *Monday mornings are waffle mornings.*

I spun. Sitting on a stool at an island counter was a man with a two-day-old shave, a ratty gray hoodie, and a cigarette burning between his lips.

Waffle Monday! Yea! He made mock jazz hands with his big knuckly meat hooks.

"Who the hell are you?"

Dead kid brother, remember? The one mommy and daddy didn't bother to name. Don't forget the little shitheads like their maple syrup heated up in the microwave. Well? Hop to it, Rachael Ray! Bus is gonna be here in a half hour.

"Give me one of those," I pointed to his cigarette.

Fuck you. I'm a figment of your imagination, and so is this cigarette. Besides, didn't you take enough from me when you starved me to death while we were still in the

130

womb? And look at you now, a fat ass crammed into a pair of yoga pants you have no business wearing with a boring job as a PA at the middle school. Not even a real teacher. A PA! Damn, Martha. Maybe I couldn'ta done any better, but I at least would have had fun trying.

My dead twin brother slipped off his stool, shuffled across the linoleum, and rooted through the cabinets.

Don't you prudes keep a single bottle of booze around this fucking joint? You trying to waste a whole life without having an ounce of fun or what?

"It's seven in the morning." The sounds of kids bitching and fighting over a bathroom came down the hall. "And I don't belong here."

My brother wasn't lying. At some point between my client's workshop and this suburban hell, I traded my jeans and leather jacket for yoga pants and a t-shirt with some bullshit school district motto about kids being the future printed across the front. Didn't matter. I left the kitchen as fast as my spin-class-ass could take me down the half-flight of stairs to the front door. There was a pair of Crocs there, just my size.

"Fuck me," I said, knowing no one ever would as I shoved my feet into those shoes.

Whoa. Watch the potty-mouth, Martha. You're in danger of pushing your PG-rated life up to PG-13, and God knows we can't have that.

There were keys hanging from a rack on the wall and an EcoBoost SUV crossover in the garage. As soon as I found my way out of the cul-de-sac maze of identical plastic houses, I headed straight for the industrial park. The sun glared in the rearview mirror, but my hangover was ancient history.

From the backseat, my brother sloshed a half bottle of brown liquid down his throat. My hand, tipped with Pinterest-fail painted-on nails clawed for the booze. "Gimme!"

He finished his pull and laughed. *You can't drink and drive! You're supposed to be the respectable one. You should be making waffles!*

The SUV swerved, and I slung it back between the lines. "You have no idea how much I need that right now."

You? Nah. You just need a good lay. You've been holding out on your man too long, and it's starting to affect your brain. Where the fuck you think you're going, anyway?

"The workshop. That transmitter. Back to the right harmonic. And when we get there, you're handing me that God damn bottle."

My palm pressed against the steel door, and it eased open with a soft and long creak.

A little B and E, huh? Now we're talking. Damn, sis. When did you stop being such a bore?

"Shut up, shut up, shut up. I made you up. You're fucking imaginary." Where was the damn flashlight app? This cell phone was a disorganized mess. How many knock-off versions of Candy Crush and Bubble Popper did it take to keep a suburbanite slob happy?

Yeah, don't remind me. I'm made up, and you're the real one. And therein lies the fucking tragedy. You ever think that mom and dad wanted a kid with a little more gumption than a soulless busy-body soccer mom?

"Take that back. I am *not* a fucking soccer mom," I whispered as we weaved through the sheetrock walls toward the workshop.

Okay. Fine. You got me. A basketball mom.

The workshop was just as I'd left it. The transmitter and spectrum analyzer right where I last saw them, still on, the screen on the analyzer still showing that green line of background frequencies and atmospheric amplitudes.

"I was here. I was standing right here, watching the spectrum. I was close to figuring something out," I told my dead twin brother as he nursed his bottle of stolen scotch. "Then…"

What are you doing, Martha? You don't have one thin idea what any of this shit does. You don't belong here. Save the cool sci-fi shit for the experts. Like me.

"I do know this shit. I… I taught eighth-grade science. The electromagnetic spectrum. Radio waves. They're no different than visible light or gamma radiation. See all these little peaks and valleys here at the bottom of the graph? It's RF. It's everywhere. In everything. From everything."

Cops are gonna find you in here. You cool with that, Missus Stepford?

The hand mic dangled off the ledge of the workbench. I was here, just minutes ago. Or was it days ago? Or maybe I was going to be here sometime in the future. Space and time, they're intertwined. If my *where* could jump, then so could my *when*. My hand wrapped around the microphone and squeezed the push-to-talk button.

"Look! Do you see it? The harmonics. That's what he was after. Those spikes repeating across the spectrum, weaker and stranger as they move away from the target frequency," I said.

Who? Who was after those squiggly lines?

"My client," I said. The words came out with false conviction as if I knew I was trying to tell a lie. "If he didn't kill the FCC man, who did?"

What fucking client? What FCC man? You mean whiny little Runt Number One and unappreciative Runt Number Two?

I turned on my brother and jabbed a finger into his stupid, macho, ephemeral chest. "I love those fucking kids and I'm about tired of hearing you talk bad about them."

Did you hear that, everybody? We got a badass over here! Fine. If you're not talking about your snot-nosed kids, then who in Christ are you talking about?

"My... My client..." My memory was slipping, like weird dreams after the alarm clock goes off. "Maybe it was me, only on some other harmonic a few skips away," I babbled, my quiet breath transmitting across thirty-five megahertz, and a little softer at seventy megahertz, and softer yet again at a hundred and five megahertz.

You're fucking losing it, sis. Maybe you do need a drink.

"Yeah. Hand me that fucking bottle already, will ya?"

I turned, my one hand still hot micing the transmitter, the other reaching towards my dead twin brother. He snickered, and as he did, he vibrated from head to toe like a weatherman on an old TV set. The harsh lights in the workshop pulsed. Everything faded in and out. My fingers stretched for the whiskey bottle. My brother dangled it out of reach, teasing me and sloshing the last two inches of booze back and forth.

The universe seemed to slosh back and forth with it. Untouchable. Intangible. Unstable. My brain flashed hot then cold. The radio played static and whined an infinite feedback loop. Then...

It was dark, and my head felt like someone had driven a railroad spike through it. Somewhere, someone turned on a light, and as dim as it was coming through the

134

cracks around a door, it hurt like hell. The ache, it almost wasn't pain but a familiar buzz letting me know I was still alive. The universal white noise that resided between my ears. The harmonics were stronger than ever. So strong I could hardly think.

"Where am I? How the fuck did I end up on the floor?"

You blacked out like a bum. Another exceptional performance from mom and dad's favorite daughter. Wait. Strike that. Only *daughter,* my imaginary dead sister said.

She always had the answers, always had a clear head, always knew the rules, and always enforced them. My own personal sheriff living right inside my head.

"Shut up. Someone is in this place with us," I whispered. I could hear them shuffle across bare concrete outside the door.

Mom and dad would be fucking ashamed, my law-and-order sister reminded me for the millionth time. *I should be alive instead of you, you know that, right? You're nothing but a fucking scumbag.*

"For all the times you've told me that, have I ever argued?" I mumbled, inebriated by the harmonics, but able to stand with the support of my office chair.

No kids. No husband. You quit the only good job you ever had and now you're nothing but a complete waste. I could have done so much better than you.

"Shush. They'll hear us," I moved toward the office's door, at first leaning on the desk and wall, but then pushing off and staggering under my own feet.

Who's going to hear? You have nobody in your life you care about, and nobody who cares about you.

"Not true. I had… a client? Kids?"

Sorry, Marie. All you ever had was a job, and you threw that away to come here. All you really have is me.

"Get out of my head. You're the reason my brain always hurts. You're the harmonic slowly killing me over all these years. You're my electromagnetic parasite."

I put my palm against the door surrounded by the thin lines of blinding light. It eased open without any resistance. Outside was a hallway made of bare sheetrock walls.

"Hello?" a man's voice echoed through the building. "I'm from the FCC. We talked over the phone."

I crept out of the office where I'd passed out. The hallway, the building, even the voice, it all sounded familiar. What the hell was I doing here, and who was this nuisance waking me up early on a Monday morning?

He already said. He's from the FCC. And you know what that means, big sis? Means you're in big fucking trouble, that's what that means.

"Go away. I should have never started talking to you. Should have left you to rot up inside mom's belly."

"Hello?" the man called out again. "This is just a routine inspection. Want to make sure you're compliant with the regs. Shouldn't take but a minute."

The hallway opened up into my workspace. Corrugated steel walls. Industrial shelving. Workbenches covered in disassembled electronics. All the component pieces of the puzzle, waiting to be assembled. The man, dressed in a checkered button-down shirt and chinos stood in the middle with his back to me. He held a metal clipboard at his hip. I slid something plastic off a nearby workbench and hefted it in my hand. The thing had the shape and weight of a brick. A big twenty-four-volt lithium-ion battery.

My imaginary dead sister laughed in the background of my brain.

"Quiet," I whispered.

You'll never get rid of me. That's what you could never figure out, Marie...

"Hello? Miss—"

My boot scraped against concrete. The man turned around.

... *I am you.*

His face... I'd seen it before. Seen it every day of my life in every mirror and stupid selfie picture. He was me, only not me. I remembered him, unshaven and bleary-eyed, standing out of place in some well-lit suburban kitchen, riding in the back seat of a nice SUV while drinking booze. Only this man was different than that man. This guy, he was sober and upstanding, with a shave so smooth it shined, but with eyes so scared they mirrored my own.

A moment hung like an asymptote balanced impossibly between up and down oscillations. We could have shaken hands. We could have run away. We could have made a hundred different decisions right then. But something about him being me, and me being him, and knowing the fear and shock boiling inside of me, and knowing that it cooked inside of him too... It was a race between who threw the first punch.

I swung the plastic brick in my hand. It made a thick dull "thonk" when it met his skull.

Stop right there! Don't! the cop in my brain called out.

The man tumbled to the ground, and I fell on top of him, too scared to do anything else but swing that battery down into his face. He begged too, almost as loud as my dead twin sister.

"Stop! No! You don't have to do this," he was saying. Or was my sister saying it? Or was it my own voice I was hearing in my head? The plastic brick made another solid connection with his skull. Blood splattered up from the impact. He flailed, and just as I hefted up the brick for another bash, he lashed out. The edge of his metal clipboard sliced across my forehead. The blood gushed down into my eyes. I toppled over, in as much pain from the gash as from the harmonic feedback blasting inside my skull.

137

I scrambled away, pawed at the blood in my eyes, and bumped against the steel cabinets below the workbenches. When the static in my brain swelled down, I came to my senses enough to wipe away the blood with my shirt sleeve.

The man from the FCC was a motionless lump on the floor. His too-familiar face lay sideways on the concrete, staring back at me with dead eyes.

What. The fuck. Have you done now?

The fire inside my skull still burned. "Not right now, sis. I respect you, and you know I love you, but for now, stay out of my fucking head," I said. Or did I? I swear the words came out of my lips, but they didn't feel like my own.

My workshop vibrated around me. The harmonics. All this was the fault of the harmonics, all the pain and noise inside my head. If I could just eliminate the harmonics...

So, in addition to being a failure, you're a murderer now. What exactly were you hoping to accomplish? said the voice of my sister who never was. A ghost living permanently in my head one or two harmonics over.

"I made you up. You're fucking imaginary."

The blood was flooding into my eyes again. I wiped with my other sleeve and that came away soaked too. My vision narrowed. The edges of everything in the workshop went blurry. Trying to get up, or maybe just trying to get a hold of something, I reached up to the top of the workbench. A pack of cigarettes tumbled off.

Those things'll kill ya, you know?

My sister, my dead sister who was only ever a wrinkled rotting fetus, walked into the room as a full-grown adult. She flickered in and out. Her hair and face changing ever so slightly with each approaching step, modulating between the uniform of a sheriff's deputy one second, jeans and a leather jacket the next, and then a t-shirt and

138

yoga pants the following. She… No… *They* stood over me, eyeing something above my head on the workbench. One of them looked down at me as I bled out and grimaced.

Mom and dad would be fucking ashamed.

There was too much blood, I knew that. No matter how much I wiped I couldn't stop bleeding. I was dying. Was dead already and dying over again. And all my sisters could do was remind me of how much I hated myself for killing them. Consciousness slipped in my grip. I slid down the metal cabinet to the floor. My dead twin brother, the man from the FCC, glared at me with those lifeless eyes a few feet away, the pool of blood around his body growing only a little faster than the pool around my body.

I should be alive instead of you, my sisters spoke in unison. *You know that, right? You're nothing but a fucking loser.*

Consciousness ebbed away, and I flailed, trying to grasp something, anything, as if life were a physical item I could cling to. Looking up, I saw the radio hand mic swinging on the end of its pigtail cord. I reached up, stretching towards the mic as if it were miles away. My fingers, wet and red, slipped through blood and batted it once, twice, then caught it and clamped down on it as if it were a slimy fish in a stream.

I didn't need to say anything. Just needed to mash down the push-to-talk button. My fingers found it and squeezed.

The universe shivered like a cold child in the winter wind. The microphone caught my rasping, dying breath. The transmitter broadcasted static, feedback, and agonal gaps on thirty-five megahertz, seventy megahertz, a hundred and five megahertz… signals cloned across the spectrum ad infinitum, each harmonic weaker than the previous. I kept my slick, wet fingers clamped around the transmit button even as my vision narrowed to a pinprick and the pressure in my veins slowed the bleeding from my head to a seep.

The universe stopped singing.

The sun was bright, but the round brim of my hat blocked out the glare and kept the reminders of my nasty affection for cheap scotch at bay. The boys from the station would be here soon enough; then they could deal with the wet work inside the corrugated steel pole barn. In the meantime, I pulled my aviators from my breast pocket and slipped them on.

Hey big brother, do you ever feel bad for them? my dead twin sister asked from over my shoulder. I turned to humor her. She was leaning against the fender of my squad car, looking smart and hip and cooler than a sister should in her tight jeans and boss leather jacket.

"Feel bad for who?" I said and padded my pockets for a pack of cigarettes.

She nodded over my shoulder to indicate what waited inside the industrial park workshop. *You know, these people you find. The ones who have clearly gone crazy. Not really their fault, is it?* Always a rebel, my imaginary sister. Always looking out for the lesser life forms of this world. She was the compassionate one our parents would have wanted to make it instead of me. But here I was, and they were stuck with me.

I guffed. "Not my problem, sis. Now where's my damn smokes?"

You're trying to quit, remember? she said. *You said you didn't want to give me second-hand cancer and kill me twice.*

"I said that? Sounds like something I would say." I think I had a pack of smoke in my squad car. In the center console maybe. "I'm a funny motherfucker, you know that?"

140

Oh, I know it, big brother. I know it.

I opened the door of my sheriff's car and started rifling through all the shit in the center console. Dispatch squawked and chirped through the radio's speaker. "I know they were in here somewhere."

Those things'll kill ya, you know?

"Yeah, sis."

I'll make you a deal, Marty. I'll tell you where you left your smokes, but first you got to tell me something.

I stopped and twisted around in the driver's seat. "What's that?"

She stood there, hip cocked out to the side, and smirked at me. *Tell me what you think they're going to find in the workshop. Better yet, tell me* who *you think they're going to find in there.*

"An engineer and some sorry sack from the FCC. What's it to you?" I said, still not finding my cigarettes.

What were their names? What did they look like when you found them in there, dead? The engineer, was he a man? A woman? How about the one from the FCC? You at least have to know his name. Was it Martin? Or maybe Mary?

I stared at her, my imaginary dead sister without a name, and couldn't for the life of me remember the answer to any of her questions.

Maybe ask them. Maybe they have your smokes.

Abandoning the search for my smokes and the squad car, I moved past her and shoved open the door to the workshop. It creaked open as I stepped inside.

Bathroom Dermatologist

First published in Horrortree on October 16th, 2022

I hate zits. I didn't ask for them. I've done everything I can to get rid of them. The creams, the rinses, the lotions, the change in diets, the gimmicks, and on and on and on. Still, they persist, regardless of my interventions. And as long as they remain, I'll be the nasty-faced teenager that no girl wants anything to do with.

God, I hate zits, but I love when they pop. The tension and the release. The pain and the relief. The wind-up and the pitch. The crescendo and the crash.

All I have to do is find the right one. So here I am in the mirror, searching and perusing, stalking and choosing the reddest of the red. The most swollen of the swollen. The tight and tender blemish. The fat wood tick. The distended roadkill along the highway. The one nine months pregnant with puss. Surely, they all connect. Like an inverse ant hill, all those mineshafts of goo twist and wind down through my skin to a central source, to a pressurized abscess, to a mother lode. If I can find the right one and pop it, all the rest of the pimples will drain out through that single tap.

Imagine the steady stream of pale gunk that will pour out of me like soft-serve ice cream.

And when it comes out, that long albino tube worm of acne, when it splats against the mirror or flops down limp onto the basin of the sink, will it only lay there, dead? Or will it rise up on its fresh but unstable foundation like a newly born foal?

And will it know its father? Its master? Its god? Without a doubt, it will obey my commands. And once commissioned, my progeny will go out into the wider world, multiplying via mitosis into broods of divergent larva. They will disperse through town, creeping through the streets along gutters and sewer lines, squirming up drain pipes into homes and bathrooms. In my premonition, I see them spreading while infecting, penetrating while writhing through flesh, manipulating while boring deep into brains. At my behest, they'll inject people with my will. My spawn will nest in the deep recesses of their minds. There, they will fester and grow and build in pressure. Then, like superheated magma, they'll rise up through cracks and fissures of the flesh until they boil up to the surface. And through my sentient pustules, I will bend the masses to my will and puppet the world. And I'll finally have some control.

I squeeze.

But God damn it. This one just isn't going to go.

The Landfill Man

First published on March 26th, 2020, in The Storyville Project, Book 2

I was a lonely landfill man, but I wasn't alone.

Sunset light seeped in through patches and slits. I rolled out of bed and staggered around my things and collections to the front door. I pushed it open, and dusk poured over me. I squinted until my squinting was done, then looked down over the dump.

This place was too crowded and busy for me all throughout the day. All the bulldozers and dump trucks, seagulls, and suburban dads with their pickups emptying so many forgotten souls. But as the sun sank and the gates locked, they all went away and left their treasures behind for me to uncover, discover, and recover.

This old single-story, two-bedroom house was the first structure built on the property. Someone, way back probably not long after World War II based on the lead pipes and asbestos walls of the house, owned this home and the land all around it. And I suppose this man, freshly returned from the war in Europe, saw people needed a place to dump the things that hurt them. So, he dug a hole and let them come here and fill it.

I figure I'm sort of the opposite of that guy. No war here, not for me. And if he wanted to help people bury their past, I was around to dig it up. That's the lesson of the landfill: Nothing is forgotten forever.

But I don't bother anybody, they don't bother me, and we like that just fine. I only go down to the commercial waste pit at night, lugging my shovel and wheelbarrow with me. They leave behind trinkets and old food, valuables and rags, their broken things and things brand new. A few years ago, someone threw away a nice headlamp because the batteries were dead, and someone else left a talking doll full of batteries because the head busted off. Now I can see at night. My shovel was a shovel with a broken handle and a rake with bent tines. My wheelbarrow used to be several wheelbarrows. Maybe the professor would say it was the same as Theseus' wheelbarrow. I think it's a new wheelbarrow, just as I'm a new and different person than who I was before.

"Tonight, we plunge through the strata," the professor said as he packed his pipe from a pouch of tobacco he cradled in his arm. "We'll delve deep through the epochs, and who knows what knowledge we'll find?"

"Or just some cans I can trade in for cash," I said as I fought to pull the wheelbarrow through the door frame.

"Ah, but in the course of digging for cans, mayhap we discover enlightenment?" the professor said.

Enlightenment, probably not. But was there more in the landfill than collectibles and recyclables? Things that would speak to me? Things with souls? I hoped so.

The professor followed me down past the warehouse of used mattresses, sponged full of urine and dead skin cells, through the barrows of old refrigerators packed full of mold, dead kids, and seeping Freon, and alongside the mountain of bicycles, some still with training wheels, some without, a few twisted and tangled and speckled with blood. The trail turned and switched back and took us deeper and deeper into the landfill. The professor followed behind me in his tweed coat and penny loafers, puffing on his pipe, one hand in his pocket, strolling straight-legged with his toes and his chin up, never afraid to step in a brackish puddle along the way. He kept quiet during our descent, his mind busier than mine, I suppose.

It was full dark by the time we reached the bottom. That was where the freshest deposits were left. The stuff still exposed and not yet buried by bulldozers. I wheeled around the garish-colored puddles of liquid until I was on the edge of the fresh trash. Then I got to work.

People think they throw things away and they're gone. They put their sins and sorrows in a bin at the end of the driveway and on Tuesday it magically disappears. Most people never even see this place. But the things they throw away are never really gone. I find their overdue bills, their porno magazines, and their shit-stained underwear. Oh, they haul it away and dump it off a cliff, cover it in dirt, but it never goes away. I find their ill-advised purchases, their financial indiscretions, their addictions. The truth is always here,

146

sometimes out in the open. Sometimes just below a thin layer of dirt. Out here, there was no lying and storytelling to make the embarrassments seem justified. There was only truth.

Layer by layer, I sifted through the forgotten and abandoned. Near the top was a framed poster of a pretty young lady in pearls and a fancy dress, smoking a cigarette with one of those long holders from the nineteen-thirties. She leaned in towards the camera, the slightest smartest smile hiding on her lips. And did she wink at me through the unbroken glass? I placed the picture into the wheelbarrow.

Here there were broken plastic toys, tiny clothes stained with baby poop and breast milk, a long knotted tube of plastic with giant pearls of dirty diapers… I was careful with the blade of my shovel around that python of piss and shit.

"Ah… the preschool era," the professor noted between puffs. "Look at all we can learn from this. The broken toys, the size of the clothes… and still in diapers. What in this young boy's life has already made him so anal-retentive do you suppose? Oh, and what do we have here? Cast aside cosmetics and creams. These are indicative of a woman who'd given up on vanity and beauty. A mother hard at work, indeed."

I moved aside the Mary Kay inventory and dug deeper. There was a wig down here. Some clothes. I picked up a head made out of Styrofoam, the kind a woman dresses up with wigs and jewelry. But it was bare, bleach-white, and blank-faced. The empty page tricked me into writing a story upon it, but I didn't like the narrative. Not one bit. So, I chucked it up to the professor's feet.

"Deeper," the professor said. "Through the ages and eras, further back in time the further down we go."

I tossed aside flattened cardboard boxes with pictures printed on them of what would be here next week. Another strata for another time. Below the cardboard were coffee grounds, rotten eggs, and those little orange prescription pill bottles. People weren't supposed to throw away medicine. It got into the groundwater and flowed into the lakes and rivers and got all the frogs and fish high. People were supposed to bring it into the sheriff's office so it could be incinerated. Turn the dope into smoke so all the birds can get high too. I don't like medicine. I got a bad history with medicine. But my shovel kept the bottles a good distance away, and they went up and out of the hole too.

Below, beer cans. Glorious, recyclable, beer cans. Dozens of them. I went about picking up each one and basketball shooting them into my wheelbarrow.

"See here," the professor said. "During this time period, alcoholics roamed the Earth."

I plucked a used needle out from between the cans and threw it up and out of the hole as far as I could. When I bent down for the next can, an empty Michelob Golden Draft Light, that Styrofoam head roamed back down into the hole and against the back of my palm. I moved and it rolled over the pill bottles and looked up at me from its place there.

"Ah… another sedimentary layer of human history," the professor whispered in awe of it. "The Epoch of Rachael. Roughly three million to, oh I'd say, four point five billion years ago."

"Fuck you, teach," I told the professor, picked the Styrofoam head back up, and threw it out at him. "She's dead. They buried her in one of those other kinds of landfills. The cute little ones outside of churches."

Rachael.

I wasn't always a landfill man, living in a landfill land. I had a real life back those three million to four point five billion years ago. Had a pretty girl of my own, and not one that just lived inside of a picture frame. Not a Styrofoam head either. I had Rachael. And Rachael had her pills. What was it that got her started on the oxies? A twisted ankle coming down the stairs? Or was it the migraines? And what was it that pushed her over the edge into heroin? The cause and effect of all those things were mixed up in my head. The sedimentary layers were all churned up and didn't lay flat in my mind anymore. But there was a vein of emotion that ran through them all, intruding up from volcanic layers to the surface.

"I loved you, Rachael."

Was that even true? I walked out the front door all the same. When the pills and drugs got too much, I left. I had to, for my own good! I had no choice. Really, I didn't. I had to let her go. I tried to wake her up that morning before I moved out. Tried to let her know. Tried not to sneak away like a thief in the night. Still, I gave up and walked out the front door and into the sun all the same.

"Dig," said the professor. "We have to discover. No matter the cost."

I dug, through time and through the ages, and the deeper I went, the more familiar it all became. Medical work scrubs with monkeys and such on them. Steel-toed boots and grease-stained jeans. Lunch boxes with ham and cheese sandwiches turned

148

green and black and flavored with penicillin. Ripped-open envelopes and papers folded three times were scattered throughout. Bills. Lots of them overdue. The license plate off our Ford Fiesta with expired tabs. The year on the little sticker didn't surprise me in the least.

"The age of overtime... difficult times... but good times..." the professor nodded and puffed.

"Good times that weren't long enough," I admitted. "I wish there were more pay stubs and fewer bills."

"There's more. More!"

When I craned my neck around to look at the professor, he was at the top of a long silo, moonlight, and stars only visible as if on the far side of a black and white kaleidoscope.

"Keep digging!" he called from above like an undertaker.

I understood I didn't have to if I didn't want to. The professor wasn't holding any grades over me, not in this school of real life. He couldn't hire or fire me. He was... He was a voice in my head. No more real than that wink from the old movie poster. I didn't want to dig deeper. Didn't need to. I was here for beer cans and unused batteries. Maybe something nice to hang on my walls. Not... this, whatever this was. But now that I was here, uncovering the things I was, I couldn't stop. Something compelled me further down. Something real. Something truthful. Something pure.

Now there were overpriced used college textbooks we never used enough. Broken computer monitors. Those old computer mice with rolling balls. Papers stained with rings of coffee. A glass pipe, very different than the professor's pipe. This layer was dusted with crumbs of marijuana and that musty smell brought me back to simpler days. I don't know when I abandoned the shovel, but I was on all fours now, pulling up the pieces of the past with my hands and bringing them to my face to inhale them in.

It didn't matter if the professor was up there on the surface, miles above my head now, calling down into the pit for me to "Dig! Dig!" I would anyway, despite things falling back in. The license plate, the contents of that uneaten bag lunch, the Styrofoam head... I pushed them aside. I was getting closer to that time, maybe the best time in my life, the moment when I knew without a shadow of a doubt that the rest of my life was going to be okay.

The strata thinned but became more detailed. An old Sublime CD measured a year. A university t-shirt was a month. A sheet of paper for each day. A strand of her hair for an hour. The moment we met. It was around here soon, and I couldn't pass it by. If I could find that, if I knew where it all began, maybe we could start fresh, together. Would I go through all the long days and fights and struggles and overtime to bring us back to the present? You're goddamn right I would.

But the present was falling back in on me. Michelob beer cans rolled down on top of the CD. A sheet of cardboard fluttered down. That framed poster of the winking rich girl landed on my back and I thrashed it off me. From millennia above, the professor knocked out the ashes from his pipe and it dusted me like a crematorium smoke stack. A pill bottle rolled and tumbled and bounced all the way down until it landed on the clothes she wore the day that had been so full of potential. Strappy sandals. A pink and yellow flower-print sundress. Big Hollywood-rehab sunglasses. I knocked the pill bottle away and buried my face in her clothes, smelling everything that was pure and wholesome the day I met my Rachael.

The nervousness. The excitement. There was magic in the air that day. When I felt the sundress swell and fill with her body, I didn't pull away. When her arms wrapped around me and pulled me in tighter, I welcomed her warmth. When the smell of her rot filled my nose and throat and lungs, I breathed in deeper. When I looked up and saw her smiling face, tears blurred my eyes. More trash tumbled down over us like blankets on our bed and I didn't mind. We let the present bury us in the past and held each other tight.

"Not letting go this time," I whispered into her ear. "I'm here for you Rachael."

Somewhere, ages and eras and epochs above us, the professor watched as the pit swallowed us whole and today's trash covered us up. He repacked his pipe, brought a match to the bowl, puff puff puffed the tobacco to life, and tossed the match over his shoulder as he strolled away.

"Interesting. All very interesting," he ruminated and rambled on.

Escape For Sale

First published on October 9th, 2023, in The Chamber Magazine

I've been here before. I'll be here again. What city or suburb is this anyway? What state? Is this Grand Rapids? Green Bay? I think Rockford, maybe. Rockford feels right.

This one is an anime convention. Teenagers in schoolgirl costumes, monster costumes, ninja costumes, animal costumes… They squeal and giggle when they spot something that delights them: an art print from their favorite show, a particularly accurate costume prop, a toy they'd been searching for, another attendee dressed up as another character from the same cartoon as them. Sales aren't going well. They're too absorbed in their own fandoms.

And what do I sell exactly? I can't tell you. Not just yet.

The other vendors put on good smiles. They engage. They recognize and complement the costumes. These small (tiny) business entrepreneurs do their best to meet these kids on their level. But… the kids in the pink and purple cutesy dog and fox outfit with the oversized paws and glossy eyes? Nobody is reaching them. Certainly, I'm not. Not with what I'm peddling.

"Alright. I give up," the vendor in the next booth says to me. She's selling knitted dolls she crocheted herself. Pop culture characters with heads and eyes like babies. I've heard her sales pitch a hundred times or more. As much as she's heard my pitch. Hers are paying off more often than mine, but not by much. She's young, energetic, and has a constant need to move and do and talk and shuffle. Whenever someone isn't at her booth, she's putting her crochet needles to work making another doll. She's perpetually on the verge of boredom. So, she takes a chance on what I have to offer.

"It's legit though, right?" she asks. The click and clack of her hooks are a constant background track to her words. "In Dubuque, I sat next to two guys at a fantasy con. They were selling magic dusts, potions, holy water, that sort of thing. The dusts were just sand and glitter. The potions were water and food coloring. I watched them fill the holy water from a bottle of Aquafina."

A good salesperson doesn't have to be crooked to be successful. Granted, many patrons wander into one of these events with no intention of making a purchase. It's the smooth words of a salesman or the glitter of something not quite gold that changes their minds. They might leave the convention center happy, thrilled even, with their new treasure, but with no idea why they bought what they had. Not my customers. Not because they're not happy with their purchase, and not because they have a firm understanding of why they made their purchase, but because they simply don't wander back out into the daylight. I don't know where they go, but I'm convinced it's further away than the parking lot.

"No. This is legit. And if it's not, well, we'll both still be here, and you can get your money back," I told her. There's no scam in my game. If there were, it would become immediately apparent. But I'm an honest salesman, and I've never issued a refund.

Dubious and curious in equal parts, she sets down her crocheting. Uncharacteristically silent, she taps her credit card to my phone. Touchless payments are all the rage at these events. The payment goes through. Rather than a refund, I provide her a talisman.

"So…" she drags out the word, holding the small object in her palm. "What now?"

I don't answer. I don't have to. She's already fading from view.

I think this is Ann Arbor, or just outside of Ann Arbor. In a mall. A comic and toy convention this time. A more diverse crowd. Overweight forty-year-old fanboys intermingle with teenage cosplayers. Innocent and unsuspecting mall walkers squint at the stranger booths. Civilian mall shoppers ask, "What is all this?" Serious collectors rifle through long white cardboard boxes for specific issues missing from their collections. I don't have to wait long to make the first sale.

I'm next to a pair of brothers who have written, drawn, inked, and printed their own comic book. They sell it as if they are carnival barkers, calling out random passers-by by the color of their clothes or what their t-shirts say. They're handing out free stickers and buttons. Hard selling, you might call it. For the most part, I ignore them.

"So, what is it?" a big-bellied man with a gray ponytail asks me. "What does it do?"

"It's escapism," I select which question of his to answer.

If he bites, this man will be my second sale of the day and of the convention, as far as I can remember. After my first sale, I was certain I'd be gone as quickly as the customer. But I remained, although I had to lean against my table to keep from fainting. I

153

think the first sale wanted to whisk me away, but I was able to stay put, grounding myself here in Ann Arbor by focusing on the feel of my table, the weight on my palms, the smells coming from the food court, and the sound of the brothers selling their comics.

"Escapism from what?"

"From everything."

He pays in cash. It's a generational difference, I've found. The older ones either pay in cash or need you to swipe their card's magnetic strip through a miniature card reader. Never Venmo or Cash App. Rarely with a tap touchless payment. The younger and hipper you are, the less likely you are to pay with cash, but as the old folks say, "Cash is king." Before the bills are under the spring-loaded metal keeper in the cashbox, and before I can pull out his change, the man with the gray ponytail has received his token and is gone.

And then, so am I.

The thing about escaping is, if you do it too much, you'll run out of things to escape from. And what you escape to becomes more and more empty. Nothing like that first high, right? If you're anything like me, soon you'll spend all your time and money chasing that Get-outta-Town dragon.

What is it I sell, you ask? Fine. I'll tell you. Baubles. Trinkets. Tokens. Talisman of Escape. Does that answer your question? No?

In Davenport, it was Davenport, I was sure of it, the Sci-fi convention has the usual blend of obsessed and dedicated disciples who only leave their cupboards for events such as these, and the curious, casual onlookers who recognize prime people-watching opportunities. Who they are doesn't particularly matter, in my case. Word of mouth travels fast, especially when the word you're selling is "Travel." But that's how it is in Davenport. People come to my table, unbeckoned, unprompted, and they each get theirs. The whole line of them. And as quickly as they make their purchases, the line disappears.

I don't mean it dispersed. It removed itself from the con and from Davenport altogether. Which begs the question, if a line begins in Davenport, where does it end?

Maybe they go to Des Moines, or Omaha, or perhaps Duluth. To another con? I don't know where they go. They never follow me to my next stop. As good of business as I've been doing, I've never had a repeat customer.

I have to fix myself to the conference center floor in Davenport just to get through the queue of eager customers. I hold onto the table and sort of stamp my feet into the thin carpet as if I'm a sailor standing on the deck of a ship in bad weather. Because I have to make the sales. I have to export my own urge to retreat, to run away, to escape, to be anywhere but here. I welcome them. I'm greedy to take their tender, no matter the form, knowing each sale fulfills some internal need while simultaneously knowing that each transaction brings me closer to the edge. So, I fix myself to this place because when I leave Davenport, and I'm beginning to doubt I'll make it through the whole line before I do, I have no idea where I might appear next.

And who I will be when I get there.

When they come and make their purchases, and when they go, eventually, so do I. Early on the tour, it only took one bauble to send me away. To sell out, I call it, even though I have plenty more trinkets to trade. I hadn't sold out of product. I sell myself out of the city. Out of one place and into another.

At the subsequent locations, it takes a little more. Two trinkets. Then three. Then half a dozen. Each time the other booths, other salesfolk, the attendees, the

155

displays… they all get thinner as I approach that tipping point. Until they're all gone. Or I'm gone. I imagine the convention continues without me, and without all those who have come and bought what I have to offer.

You know how they say in AA meetings, "If an addict gets on a bus in Boston bound for Chicago, an addict will get off that bus in Chicago"? That's their way of saying a change in location doesn't mean a change in the person.

I never imagined that the bus was so crucial to that chain of events. Because when I travel, sans bus, fading out of a civic center in Davenport and fading into a National Guard armory in Lansing, I'm not quite the same self I was in Davenport. I am myself. It's just the person who was in Davenport isn't quite me anymore. I am in Lansing. More so than I had been in Davenport. This is a bookseller's convention. I am beset on all sides by independently published authors of varying degrees of talent, and I have no books to sell. Regardless, when I move a dozen of my talismans, clutching the lip of my table for the last handful of patrons, and I arrive in St. Paul, I am more in St. Paul than I had ever been in Lansing. My present always trumps my past. The here is always more concrete than the there. The moment is always stronger than memories. Consciousness is always more real than dreams.

In St. Paul, it's a horror convention. There are movie screenings. There's a costume contest. There's a class on DIY practical effects for all the budding Tom Savinis standing on the plastic drop cloths the convention center staff rolled out to catch all the corn syrup and food coloring. There's a "Scream Queen" contest to see which lady can belt out the best banshee wail. There are autographs and Q&As and meet and greets of men whose faces never touched the silver screen because they were always hidden behind the masks and make-up of the monsters they played.

I'm in the vendor's hall. In artist's alley. To my right is a taxidermist who takes dearly departed forest creatures and turns them into horror movie murderers. He has a Pinhead porcupine, a Freddy Krueger ferret, a Michael Meyers muskrat, and a skunk in a Friday the 13th hockey mask. The lack of alliteration between Jason Vorhees and the skunk stands out only because it's so ubiquitous among the rest. Nevertheless, the artistry is impeccable. Not for everyone, but here at this convention? The taxidermist has found his target audience. To my left is a sweet old woman who is selling hand towels and dresses patterned in the Universal Studios classic monster line-up. Dracula. Frankenstein. The Invisible Man. The Mummy. The Invisible Man. The Creature from the Black Lagoon. The Wolfman. She had a hip Elvis meets Elvira rockabilly style. Jet-black beehive hair. Over-the-top makeup. Thick-framed, winged spectacles. Platinum black flats with frilled white socks. Spiderweb patterned leggings. A poodle-skirt with a dancing skeleton instead of a dog at the end of the leash.

My table, in comparison, is as blank and boring as a white cotton bedsheet in an S&M boudoir. I have my cash box. I have a miniature card reader that plugs into my phone. I have a small music box in which I store my tokens. It plays Für Elise if I ever wound it up. I don't. I have a small sign that reads "Escape for Sale," and the prices, which I feel are very reasonable. Nothing more. No big banners or displays. Just me, the means of payment, and the product.

It was the third day of the con and both the rockabilly seamstress and the twisted but talented taxidermist act like we've already gotten to know each other. Somehow, I've already earned their trust. As if I'd been sitting next to them, pitching and hawking my wares, since the con began.

It makes sense in some ways. I don't remember loading in and setting up. And I never tear down and load out. Wherever I go, my table is set up and ready for business. I appear at each venue as neatly and cleanly as I disappear. My customers come with no prelude, and I leave without epilogue. Nevertheless, my things are here before I arrive. Do they remain after I'm gone? Do I remain, in some outdated, no-longer-precisely-me version of who I had been? Is there already a version of who I will become getting to know the next pair of neighboring vendors at the next con?

My neighbors, all of them, from the restless doll maker in Rockford to the comic book brothers in Ann Arbor, to the hack novelists in Lansing, to these two eccentric horror fiends, they have known me. And maybe I know them too. I know their products and their spiels. If I tried, if I plunge the memories I have no right to have, I suspect I might be able to conjure up a name or a hometown. That possibility scares me. It feels intrusive for me to try. Like trespassing. And that feeling, that sense that trying to remember things before I arrived here is an invasion of someone else's land leaves me suspicious that someone else had been here before I arrived. Someone whom those memories belonged to. Someone who wasn't me. Not even a part of me. Until they were all of me. Or I was all of them. And then suddenly I am more them than they had ever been.

After all, the now always wins over the then.

As my customers slip away, into the ether or maybe to another con in Peoria, Kansas City, or Springfield, my neighbors never notice their absence. Even when a large pack of loud Twilight vampires comes down the aisle, skip the dresses and hand towels, stop at my table, and never make it to see the Woodchuck Chucky on display at the next table over.

I'm selling more now, lasting longer and longer at each show. I'm remaining more me at each stop. I'm unloading more and more of my escapism on them.

And that leaves me with what? When I truly sell out of my baubles, trinkets, tokens, and talismans, what will I have left? The prices are, as I said, very reasonable, which means the touchless transfers and the cold hard cash in the metal box don't add up to much. Enough for a few nights in a local hotel and a few meals. I haven't used the money, not since starting out on tour. Money was never the point. So, when I sell out, not out of the vendor's hall in St. Paul, but sell out of escapes, what will I have to show for it? Persistence? Permanence? Imprisonment? Will I be able to pack up my things and walk out the backdoor like all the other dealers? They, no doubt, have vans and trailers to load up their tables and collections of comics, toys, props, and products to haul to the next stop. I'm unaware of any van or car waiting for me beyond the loading docks. Will I be stranded wherever I run out of inventory, be it here in St. Paul or at the next stop? Where will I go after the convention closes its doors? I don't remember the last time I wasn't at a con, when I wasn't perfecting my pitching and hawking my wares for the tap of a card or a few more paper presidents. My last Monday felt like eons ago. Can I even exist outside of conference halls, strip malls, and community centers? Have I ever? In here, working my table, making sales, I am me. But out there? Suddenly, my dwindling supply becomes all the more valuable. Precious even. Priceless, as in whatever cash or card the next customer presents won't come close to tipping the scales.

"You've slowed down," the seamstress with the gaudy purple eyeshadow and violent red lipstick tells me. "For a while there, you didn't have a break!"

"It's Sunday," The taxidermist interjects. "It always slows down on Sundays."

"Clark Kent Day," I say.

"Huh?" the seamstress says.

"On Friday and Saturday, they come in full regalia. Each one of them dressed as their own version of Superman," I say. I don't remember where I picked up on this notion. If I had to guess, I'd say in Ann Arbor at the comic and toy convention. "By the time Sunday rolls around, they've scrubbed away their make-up. The big costumes have been traded for sweatpants or pajamas. All the Supermen are gone. Only Clark Kents remain. Still, don't count Clark Kent out. On Superman Days, Saturdays, or even Fridays if you're lucky, you make your table back. On Clark Kent Days is when you make your profit."

My neighbors nod and I know they'll incorporate my vocabulary into theirs. Sundays will be Clark Kent Days for them for every future weekend spent at a con.

"Your table has been lively though," the seamstress gestures to my spartan setup.

"Wouldn't know anything about that," Stan (Stan! The taxidermist's name was Stan.) says. "I don't work with the living."

We laugh at that, having fun with the idea of this man only interacting with those who have passed on, and those who have passed on being small woodland critters.

I like these two. Quirky, but still relatable and real. Neither too full of themselves or too aggressive with the old hard sale. Amiable. Funny. Kind. I know, even though I've never stayed until the end, come the close of the convention, we'll trade business cards and find each other on social media, and hope to run into each other at the next pit stop along the highway. After all, as Evelyn (The rockabilly dressmaker's name is Evelyn, of course, it's Evelyn, it has always been Evelyn,) says, "It's a small world."

Her question remains unasked but waiting for an answer all the same. Why had my sales dropped off so sharply when the two of them were still doing, at least, moderate business?

I pull the unwound and silent music box close to me, away from any potential buyers. Not on display. Not anymore. I peek inside and count the small supply within.

160

"What is it again, exactly, you're selling?" Evelyn asks. "I've heard you describe it, but I don't think I quite understand."

"Nothing," I lie, too sharply. "Honestly, it's a sort of participator placebo. A token with the imaginary power to assist the imagination. Snake oil for the overactive mind. Nothing of value."

"I'll take it," Stan says with such affirmation he can't be denied.

"No. I couldn't. You guys are–"

"I insist," Stan says and comes out from his booth to the front of mine. "A mental tool, imagined to help the imagination? How can I say no to something like that?"

"It is very intriguing," says Evelyn. "Me too. I want one too."

There were four left when I counted them. If I make this sale, there will only be two left. My fun, funny, quirky, honest, talented, and relatable neighbors will be gone. And will the remaining pair of talismans be enough to send me after them? Or will I be stuck here on the streets of St. Paul to face the dull and drab realities of a Monday morning with no neighbors, no products, no customers, no sales, and no convention? The thought sends my nerves shaking my bones.

Stan the taxidermist drops his cash on my table. Enough for two trinkets. The old-school method of contactless payment. And as soon as the money lands on my table, my two new friends and two more of my talismans disappear.

I'm alone, and I'm in dire short supply of escapes.

"So… what are you selling?" a kid in zombie make-up asks. He shows no signs of noticing the empty booths flanking me, or my suddenly estranged previous customers. All he knows is that I have something people want. And if people want it, then he absolutely has to have it.

"Loneliness," I tell him. "And I'm all out. Now beat it."

161

Taken aback, no doubt unaccustomed to the eternally gregarious vendors eager for his weekly allowance, he fades into the crowd. Lost in the masses until I can't see him anymore, but he's not disappeared. Only paying customers earned the right to slip through the bars of this cell.

Checking up and down the row, and seeing that, indeed, Clark Kent Day had thinned the crowd, I ease my grasp on the music box. I surely can't keep the last two baubles in my inventory forever. But I don't know how to restock. I don't know where I got my initial supply. My preparation for these conventions was as far away as the last Monday. Eau Claire, Fort Wayne, Cedar Rapids, Dayton, even Bismark are infinitely closer than wherever it was I had begun. Would it end here, in St. Paul? I let go of the music box and crack open the cash box. The tray to the far right, President Jackson's tray, is moderately full, but not nearly as full as the far left tray where all the Washingtons make their home. And what about the online account? Is there enough in there to buy me a plane or a bus ticket back home? If I can even remember where back home is? I open the app.

Before I can see the balance, a bank card obscures my view. Blue stars like fireflies burst on the display. The tap transfer has gone through, adding a measly amount to the balance. Looking up, I see the already thinning visage of the boy in zombie garb, more ghost than undead now. If his wily smile wasn't so bright, I don't think I'd see him at all.

Then he is gone, and my second to last talisman is gone with him.

I all but tackle the music box, clamp it shut with the little hasp, and tuck it on my lap, under the table. I twist the key to the cash box, sealing it from further business. I close the app on my phone and then power it down altogether. Perhaps closing the app was enough. Certainly, airplane mode would have prevented any transfers from going through. But I can't allow any more sales. Not today. Perhaps never again.

From down the aisle, a mother is calling out for her son. "Joe? Joe! Where'd you go?"

Did Joe arrive on Clark Kent Sunday in full zombie attire? If so, would he arrive on Superman Saturday somewhere else in the same get-up?

And what about me? If I sell my last item to the next enthusiastic patron who wanders up, will it be enough to send me away from this place? If it is, where will I land next? Lincoln? Sioux Falls? Waterloo? Columbus? Fargo? Akron?

There is only one way to find out. I never make any purchases at these conventions. Always been my mission to fill the cash box rather than take from it. The money isn't really my money anyway. It's the business' money. Buying my last bauble with that money wouldn't really be buying it at all. The few bills in my wallet on the other hand...

I cracked open my old, leather trifold. A single, worn-thin, dollar bill rests in the crevice. Usually, a talisman goes for much more than this, but I think the time is right for a Going Out of Business sale. I pluck the lone bill from my wallet and unlock the cash box. With Washington still clutched tightly in my fist, I lift the metal arm holding all the other singles in place.

Wherever my last token takes me, that is where I will stay. One final escape from which I can never escape again.

"Go ahead, buddy," I speak to myself, or the person I will have been once I leave here. "Loneliness is on sale."

The dollar drops into the cash box, and I am gone.

Where Universes Go to Die

First published in February 2023 in Teleport Magazine

When the universes came to an end, their Gods gathered to discuss. I hid and watched and listened.

Where I hid changed based on how they conceptualized this nexus of potential future universes. In truth, there was nothing. How could there be anything outside of their universes? Where can a God exist outside their creation? After all, weren't these four turtles the ones at the bottom of the stack?

But they conceptualized the nexus in a manner consistent with their creations. When Alpha addressed Sigma, Epsilon, and Zed, they were old rich men smoking expensive cigars in a Fifth Avenue penthouse. They wore designer suits and ties and uncomfortable shoes. They sat in overstuffed leather chairs and gazed out the wall of windows onto a foggy Center Park. I was a woman, a young paralegal who wasn't supposed to be on the other side of a cracked door, eavesdropping on this boy's club conversation.

"It started the same way all universes start," Alpha said, sauntering over the thick carpet, taking his time to inhale and exhale a thick cloud of cigar smoke. "I said,

165

'Let there be light,' and there was light. And naturally, I moved on to the creations from there."

"And?" Sigma asked, dubious.

"They worshiped me, fellas," he said. "Thought of me as someone they could talk to. Someone who would actually listen to them and change the course of their existence based on their pleas. There were trillions of them! And most of them actually believed that I paid specific attention to each individual, as if they weren't a collection of infantalisms. Eventually, I just didn't want to deal with it anymore, the contractual obligation to provide such personal interactions. What it came down to was disappointing them perpetually or disappointing them once and for all and ending it. So, I did the only reasonable thing."

"Oh my god!" Epsilon, suddenly a teenage girl, gushed. We were no longer in a Manhattan penthouse smoking imported cigars. Now, we were in Epsilon's construct: a suburban bedroom late at night. They were girls in pajamas all sitting crisscross applesauce on a big bed, surrounded by pillows and candies and make-up and pop music. "Like, creations can be so immature, am I right?"

"Tell me about it," Alpha rolled her eyes at the very thought of creations.

"Get a load of this," Epsilon said. "My creations? They didn't even know me. And you will not believe this. They each thought they were God."

"No way," Zed said, most of her attention paid to her toenails she was painting.

"As if," Sigma, indignant, said.

"Oh my god," Alpha laughed.

I was a younger boy, hiding in a closet, peeking through the slates in the door, hoping to see them in their underwear, fighting with pillows, or maybe practicing kissing with each other.

Meanwhile, Epsilon carried on. "Like each one of them. This one thought he was God above all the rest. This one? Also thought she was God above all the rest. They had some pseudo-science justification for it, like, something about the superpositions of quarks and their, like, complete inability to grasp decoherence at the quantum level. Like, seriously. I couldn't even."

"For reals! How self-centered and needy can creations be, right?" Zed said.

"I know, right. Like, how pathetic," Epsilon said. "I had to end it. I mean, I just had to. For their own good."

"Okay, but check this out," Zed said, still dabbing neon pink paint onto her toes. Then, before the next words were out of her mouth, we were transported out of Epsilon's conceptualization and into Zed's.

It was still night. We were still in some made-up city. Still conceptualized as creations of these Gods. Only the details changed. They were slightly older, on the borderline of what their creations might call adulthood. They were sitting on the hoods of cars in a massive parking lot outside of a concert venue. All the other concert-goers had gone home. One car was broken down, but they were in no rush to have it fixed. The place was quiet and still. They were high, passing a joint from one to the other to the other to the other and back again. Their ears still rang from the concert. They were relaxed, unsuspecting, at peace.

"My creations… they almost didn't believe in any gods," Epsilon said, his hazy words dragged out slowly. "They had this far out idea that, like, in some ways they were gods, but only in a summation sort of way. As if, together, all of them combined, they were the universe and the universe itself was God. And not just the highest level of my creations. Not just the humans, but animals and plants and the smallest microbes. They all combined to form the universe, and as a whole of their parts, they were God. There was no death. No birth. Just a continuous cycle of life energy coming together in a body, and then dissipating to rejoin the rest of the energy and to be reorganized in some other life form later on."

"You gave 'em shrooms, didn't you, you son of a bitch," Beta said, another stoner amongst stoners.

"Maybe I did. Maybe they gave it to themselves. Maybe it was just what the universe wanted," Epsilon said.

"Gnarly," Zed said, another stoner amongst stoners now.

"And as they all understood themselves to be pure life, pure energy, I became pure life and pure energy. We coalesced as one. My universe, my creation, myself... We didn't so much end as collapsed inwards upon the weight of our own love. We imploded in one all-inclusive beautiful eternal death."

"I can dig it," Alpha said and blew out a big cloud of dank smoke towards the heavens.

I could not. Dig it, that is. In another car, unmarked, borrowed from the impound lot, I sat in the dark, watching and listening. My uniform was back at the station, but my badge and cuffs and gun were tucked neatly under my flannel shirt. I could take them all down if I wanted to. Bust 'em and confiscate their weed. Drag them by their ears to the station. Get this all sorted out downtown. If I wanted.

"Sigma?" Epsilon said, and for an instant, they were girlfriends at a sleepover again. "What about your universe? Did they worship you? Despise you? Dish! Girl! Spill the tea!"

Sigma blew a bubble, and before it popped, we were all back in the penthouse. The pink gum transmuted to tobacco smoke mid-exhale. Above us, cigar smoke hung like a pall. Below us, Central Park was submerged in an ocean of mist. I pressed the rim of a glass against the oak door and peered through the crack a little further. Sigma considered the surroundings, as luxurious as it was, but shook his head. The tobacco smoke was marijuana smoke. They were back on the hoods of cars. I spied on them from a darkened driver's seat, my gun uncomfortably pressing into my hip. Sigma sat up from the car hood, looked to Alpha, Epsilon, and Zed, then dismissed this construct as well with a wave of his hand.

We were in a lecture hall. A big one hidden deep in the innards of an old and prestigious campus. Designed more like a concert hall than a modern conference center, there were curtains at Stage Left and Right, massive chandeliers overhead, and distant seats hidden up in the shadows. That's where I sat, in the back, far away from the podium and stage lights. Alpha, Epsilon, and Zed sat centered in the front row. Sigma was up front. She wore business slacks, heels, and a pristine white laboratory coat. Before her wasn't just a podium, but a long laboratory table with a stainless steel sink and gas assemblies. On it were various three-ring binders opened to charts, graphs, and scientific findings. There were beakers and graduated cylinders, a microscope, slides, and petri dishes. Sigma wore thick black-rimmed glasses and a small microphone clipped to her lab coat.

"My creations held onto no such superstitions and ridded themselves of those sorts of spiritual inclinations. Data was their god, more so than myself," Sigma said. "They examined their surroundings and experiences, recorded them, evaluated hypotheses against them, and found the machines inside the ghosts. For every effect there was a cause. For every mystery, an answer. For every problem, a solution. After only a handful of millennia, they'd reached their zenith. No war. No disease. No hunger. No hate. Instead, peace. Perfection. And without conflict, there was nothing left in them that interested me. So, I ended it, dispassionately and thoroughly, without pain or hardship, but definitively and eternally. And so it goes."

Alpha, Epsilon, and Zed scribbled down notes and flipped through text books. Epsilon, having found no answers in the book in front of her, hesitantly raised her hand.

"Miss Sigma," she began. "When you said they ridded themselves–"

A textbook slid off my thighs and onto the floor. It smacked flat and loud against the concrete. I didn't realize I even had textbooks in my lap. An old frayed-edged notebook followed the thick book, rattling through the air like dried leaves. I froze, statue-stiff.

"What was that?" Alpha asked.

They all turned back my way.

And I was inside the closet, behind the slats, peeping at the girls in their pajamas.

"Omega, if that's you, you little turd sniffer!" Epsilon threatened from the bed.

My name wasn't Omega. That was part of her conceptualization. They had no word for my name. All the same, I pushed back deeper into the closet, and when I did, my head bumped into a row of wire clothes hangers. They chimed harmonically. The girls scrambled up from the bed like alerted jet fighters.

Then the door to the penthouse eased open against my weight. The glass I had pressed against it slipped from my fingers and shattered against the berber. I stood there, wholly visible and vulnerable in the doorway. All four of them slowly turned their heads my way. Alpha, Sigma, Epsilon, and Zed, each of them taken aback by the interruption.

"Omega, my dear," Alpha said. "What do you think you're doing here?"

I turned to flee, to run from the penthouse and escape. It wasn't too late to save… well, to save everything. But as I left the penthouse, I spilled out of the bedroom closet in a tangle of laundry and forgotten play things. As I picked myself up, I saw the auditorium's exit at the top of the stairs was blocked by Sigma in her lab coat and glasses. Epsilon waited in front of the other set of doors across the seats. Alpha and Zed crept up the steps from below, hands held out like claws ready to catch me. Then, in a flash they were surrounding my unmarked squad car. Their hands slapped against the glass. Fingers jabbed and thunked and pressed. They rocked the car back and forth on its suspension. They yelled and spat and let me know in no uncertain terms that they knew who I was.

Only, they didn't.

If they did, maybe they wouldn't have behaved so aggressively.

Zed put his hands on my shoulders and guided me over the broken glass and into the penthouse with its magnificent view of Central Park in the misty distance.

"You've been hiding, Omega," Alpha said, when I was brought before him. "Did you really think we'd never discover you? Speak up!"

He didn't know what he was asking for, but then again, neither did any of his multitudes of faithful worshipers. The masses he brought into existence only to serve as his slaves. Those small petty creations. They didn't know what they were dealing with.

These small petty creations drew closer around me. So confident were these men in their expensive business suits and leather shoes and suspenders and rich cigars. Like bullies on a playground, they stood over me, looking down on me from all four sides. But all that was a construct. A conceptualization. Perhaps if they weren't so lost inside their own heads they would have seen more clearly. But such is the disease of Gods, and I had the only cure. It was time to knock the turtles off their stack.

"Now that everything's out in the open," Alpha said, "what do you have to say for yourself?"

"Let it end," I said, and it did.

171

Everything. It all ended. The four Gods were gone, wiped from existence as if they never were. As were the remains and memories of their creations and the seeds of their next creations. Even their constructs. No New York City penthouse. No suburban bedroom. No dark and sparse parking lot. No old lecture hall. When I erased them, I erased their ideas too. After all, if I was to start fresh, how could I leave any of their history behind to taint the future?

For a moment, I swam, without form, size, or limits in an eternal expanse. A vacuum so complete it betrayed all those rules Sigma had thought she'd discovered, so full of potential it was inconceivable to Epsilon's expanded mind, so sacred that all of Alpha's creations weren't enough to praise its glories, so satisfying that it dwarfed the contentment of all of Zed's self-assured mini-God creations. I was alone. I gave the emptiness its time. A minute and a millennium were all the same here in this nexus. But inevitably, I had to start over again.

I returned to my own construct, and did I flavor it in the stylings of their creations? Perhaps. I strolled across a comfortable room in a humble cabin surrounded by endless acres of woods. Soft snow was landing on the boughs of pine trees outside my window. There was a big desk in front of a broken-in chair. A ceramic coffee mug steamed amongst knick-knacks, curiosities, stacks of paper, cups of pencils, reference books, and the usual desk clutter. Centered before the chair was an old Multivac typewriter. A blank paper was already rolled in, awaiting my first keystroke. I sat down.

Where to begin? Where to begin?

I was just leaning into the typewriter, had just laid the tips of my fingers on home row when something cracked from outside of the office. Like a startled deer, I twisted to look for its source.

The door to the office was only partially open and gave me a limited view of the cabin's main room. There was a couch and chair surrounding a fireplace. It was probably just the burning wood that had popped and given me a start. Nothing to be concerned with.

Now, where to begin?

My fingers found their life, and I hammered out the first line, "Let there be light," and there was light.

Humanzees

Never before published

I shuffled into the room along with the others. It wasn't a big room, and it was only lit by a single fluorescent light directly above the table. The door, the walls, and anything a foot beyond the table were draped in darkness. Just a table, six chairs, one for each of us, and a scattering of objects on the table. Notepads and pencils, pre-packaged snacks, and those little water bottles no taller than a fist high. We made our way into the light, pulled the chairs from the table, and took our seats.

It was clear from the start that they were looking to cover the demographics when we were selected to be a part of this focus group. There were three females and three males, two young, two middle-aged, and two elderly, one of each gender of each age group. The middle-aged woman was visibly pregnant, ready to pop any day. Her eyes met mine and acknowledged me as her cohort, both of us being of the same age group. Hers weren't the only ones that gave away the workings behind them. We were all lonely, aimless folks. I could see it in our collective eyes, but perhaps more in hers than all the rest. When she sat down next to me, she had to sit further back to give her belly room, but not far from my elbow. The younger woman, full of energy, hopped into her

174

chair while the elderly folks had to exert a little more effort to get comfortable in their seats. The young man, hardly a man, as close to being a boy as the woman next to me was close to being a mother, he grabbed one of the little packages of fruit snacks and went about fighting with the wrapper to get it open.

"Anybody have any idea what this is all about?" the old man said, scratching his beard.

"I suppose they'll tell us," the old woman said, also scratching an itch. Hers behind her ear.

We didn't wear any name tags. We were all strangers to each other. Anonymous. Unattached. Indifferent. I suppose they planned it that way.

"I mean, they're paying us so… does it matter?" the young woman said.

A TV flickered to life in the gloom behind mine and the mother-to-be's backs. We turned around and followed the gaze of the others.

A woman, only visible from the chest up, moved into frame. She was odd-looking, but very beautiful and professionally dressed. She had large eyes but a tiny mouth. Her skin was nearly as pale as the white wall behind her. She stood stiff-backed with her bulbous eyes set forward.

"Good morning, everyone," the woman said, her pleasant voice coming through speakers hidden in the shadows. "Thank you for volunteering for this important research study. Your opinions are very important to us."

"We are getting paid, right?" the young woman asked.

"Can they even hear us?" the old man asked. "Hey! Can you even hear us in here?"

"Oh, calm down for heaven's sake," the old woman said, as if she were the old man's long-suffering wife. But they weren't husband and wife. I could tell by the smell of them.

"You gonna tell us what this is all about?" the young man, still trying to open the package of fruit snacks, said.

"The six of you have been selected to participate in this focus group specifically because of your lack of previous knowledge on this significant issue. This ensures that you will approach the topic from an unbiased position. I will give you a brief history of the subject matter, and you will be given three courses of action from which each of you must choose one," the woman on the TV said, unphased by the banter in the room or the endless crinkling of the package in the young man's hands. "Your votes don't need to be unanimous, but we are requiring you to stay in the room until a simple majority has been found."

Six of us, three options, the first option with three votes wins, I thought but didn't say.

"Allow me to begin," the woman on the TV said and then proceeded to read from a script. "Humans and chimpanzees share ninety-five percent of their DNA sequences. As early as the nineteen twenties, scientists inside the Soviet Union conducted experimentations on the potential of cross-breeding humans and chimpanzees. They were, however, unsuccessful in creating any living specimens."

"Wait. What?" the young woman piped up. The dismay and disgust were painted on her face.

Unphased, the woman on the TV continued. "Throughout the twenty-first century, other private entities and nation-states conducted their own experiments on the hybridization of humans and chimpanzees. Most notable, The People's Republic of

China, whose scientists were able to successfully impregnate three female chimpanzees with human spermatozoa. The study was stopped, however, for what was cited as ethical reasons. The participating scientists were sent to labor camps and the pregnant chimpanzees, along with their potential offspring, died from neglect."

At that, the room sort of lost its cool, if it had any to begin with. The young woman let out a long and strained, "Oooooh my gaaaawd!" The old man smacked the surface of the table. The young man threw the unopened package of fruit snacks at the TV and missed. The pregnant woman held her belly as if it were a ball in a game of keep-away. The old woman stated plainly, "I don't want any part in this."

The woman on the TV went on as if the old man's suspicions were right and she couldn't hear a decibel of our ruckus. "We here at Dotty Paradigm Genetics are proud to say that we have achieved what others could not. We have successfully bred and maintained a small population of human-chimpanzee hybrids, patented and traded marked as Humanzees. As all Humanzees are our genetic creations, Dotty Paradigms holds all intellectual property rights of our Humanzees."

At that, the young woman shrieked, actually *shrieked*, at the TV.

"We, at the corporate leadership level of Dotty Paradigms, are highly aware and concerned with the wider public's opinions and reactions to the products we create. And that's where you come in," the TV woman said in her slick-as-butter happy tone. "This focus group's votes will determine Dotty Paradigm's future actions on this highly sensitive matter. Again, we thank you for your participation and encourage you to take on your responsibilities with the utmost earnesty. Once you are presented with the three courses of action, please discuss your thoughts and opinions with the group. As a group, you will be allowed to ask three questions. After your questions have been answered, and you've had sufficient time to debate, you will be required to find a simple majority.

Again, the decision of the simple majority will determine the future actions of Dotty Paradigm Genetics. Here are the three courses of action of which you must select one.

"Option One: Humanzees are beautiful living creatures and should be afforded the opportunity to live and procreate as they wish.

"Option Two: Humanzees are a crime against nature. Those currently living should be allowed to live, but they should not be allowed to procreate, and Dotty Paradigms should produce no additional Humanzees.

"Option Three: Humanzees are an abomination and should be exterminated immediately and regardless of any other factors." Her voice even managed to make the word *abomination* sound as sweet as cherries.

"Please select a spokesperson who will present the group's three allowed questions and inevitably tally the votes that will decide the fate of Dotty Paradigms' IP, The Humanzees. Thank you again for your careful consideration on this matter."

With that, the TV winked out, and we were left in that pool of light around the table.

I couldn't believe what I'd heard, and couldn't believe that the smooth-talking, smooth-faced, small-mouthed, pale-skinned, big-eyed woman on the TV left us the way she had. I was slow to turn back to the center of the table, thinking that she had to reappear on the TV and explain herself and for that matter, the company she worked for, at least a little more than she had. When I finally swiveled my chair back to the table, I found the other five members of the focus group all sitting quietly with a fingertip touching their noses.

"Son of a–" I began.

"Nose-goes, dude," the young man said. "You're our spokesperson."

I should have expected such nonsense from the younger generation, but the elderly and the pregnant?

"First of all," the old man said, "I don't believe a word that woman said."

"You think it's all fake?" the young woman said. "They couldn't have actually–"

"Oh, I believe they did it," the old man said. "And that's about all I believe."

"How horrible?" the old woman said. "Aren't there laws concerning such things?"

"Killing animals, sure," the young man said, grabbed another package of fruit snacks, and resumed his ongoing struggle with wrappers. "But you heard her. These Humanzees? They're intellectual property. Same as like… the words in a book or the code in a video game."

More outbursts and exclamations followed that. I, on the other hand, pinched a pencil in my fingers and slid a notepad in front of me. If I were the focus group's spokesperson, I suppose I had certain responsibilities. And the sooner I got around to them, the sooner this whole travesty would be over. I wrote three categories at the top of the notepad: Life, No Kids, and Death. I drew two vertical lines, separating the three categories into columns, and set the pencil down. Then I waited for the others to calm down so I, the spokesperson, could speak.

"Okay, everyone. What questions do we want to ask them?" I finally addressed the table.

"Can we leave?" the young woman said. "I thought this was going to be like a Coke versus Pepsi sort of thing. Not… Not *this*."

"They already said," the young man began, but interrupted himself by turning his focus to the little package of fruit snacks. "We can't leave…" struggling, "...until we

179

make…" more struggling, "... a decision." And finally, he managed to open the package, albeit, with a little too much strength and zeal. The little jellied fruits went flying across the room and bouncing off the table, off the pregnant woman's belly, onto the floor, and into the darkness.

"Well, if none of us want to be here, we should make this easy on ourselves and choose to let those poor creatures be," the old woman said.

"You're not suggesting we allow those monstrosities to exist and multiply, are you?" the old man snapped back. They really could have been husband and wife, grandpa and grandma still living together after a whole lifetime spent at each other's throats. "They're an affront to human decency."

"Yeah but are they an affront to *Humanzee* decency?" the young man laughed at what he thought was a fantastic joke.

"I say we kill them all and be done with it," the old man said. "They're a thing that never should have been."

"What a horrible thing to say!" the old woman fired back.

On my notepad, I made one tick mark under "Life" and one under "Death."

"No, I'm with Grandpa," the young woman said. "We need to make them extinct. Like, yesterday."

I made a second tick mark under "Death."

"Well, I never!"

The young man had managed to recover one of the fruit snacks and was holding it up to the light as if it were Yorick's skull. "Can't we just, like, hang with them? I mean, I kind of want to meet one. Maybe they could play video games with us and just chill. We might vibe together. We could each have our own little monkey-man to hang with."

"What, like a pet?" the young woman said.

180

When I first saw the two of them, both attractive and about the same age, I figured they might leave here with each other's numbers. Now, I was realizing that if the young man ever had a shot, he'd blown it. Reclining back, he tossed the gummy up in the air, arcing it toward his open mouth. It bounced off his brow and joined the others in the darkness.

"Listen, do we have any questions we want to ask them?" I interrupted. "I don't want to be here anymore than any of you. Let's just get to it. Sound good?"

"This is a whole species of living beings," the old woman said. "How can all of you be so flippant?"

"I'm fine with whatever," the pregnant woman spoke up for the first time. Her expression was an aloof mask, but she was pretty. In a familiar way. In a way opposite to the woman on the TV. "Just so long as they're not allowed to have children."

The young man laughed once and loudly at that. "You're one to talk."

"Motherhood is a precious thing," the mother-to-be next to me said. "Human motherhood, I should say. And what happens if a chimpanzee gives birth to a human? Would you really allow that?"

I made a mark under the center column, the one labeled, "No Kids," on my notepad.

"I don't think that some of them are human, and some are monkeys," the young woman said. "I think they're all both human and monkey."

"Ape, actually," the young man corrected her, even though he'd been the first to introduce the term "monkey" to our little huddle. "Chimpanzees are members of the great ape family, so they're not monkeys. That's how come they don't have tails. Just like humans don't have tails."

"How enlightening," the old man drolled.

"Well, some of them are certainly more human than chimpanzee. And I bet others are more chimpanzee than human," the pregnant woman said.

"Animals," the old man said. "They're either humans or they're animals. And we can't possibly allow that line to be blurred. And that is why we absolutely need to kill each and every one of them as soon as possible. My vote stays the same."

I circled the tally mark under the "Death" column on my notepad. Before saying, "But what about the questions? Do we want to ask them any questions?"

"Oh, I have like, a million questions, bro," the young man said, reaching for another bag of treats.

"Will you stop that!" the old woman said. "Put those down. That crinkling is going to drive me insane!"

"What questions–" I began but was cut off. If this troop of ours had any collective traits, patience wasn't one of them.

"Like, how smart are they? Can they talk?" the young man asked. "Do they even want to be alive?"

"Of course, they want to be alive!" the old woman snapped. "Humans want to be alive. Chimpanzees want to be alive. For heaven's sake, even dogs and cats and mice want to be alive."

"Well, yeah, sure. But can they tell us they want to be alive?" the young man said.

"What difference does that make?" his generational cohort yelled back at him. "I'm sure serial killers all beg for their lives from the electric chair right before we throw the switch, but that doesn't–"

"Okay! Fine! But can they tell us whether or not they want to have kids?" the young man fired back at the young woman. "Maybe they'd be happy just to, you know, chill with us for a while."

"So, you're in favor of not allowing them to procreate?" the pregnant gal next to me asked him.

"I mean, I guess, sure," the boy said. He had set the bag of treats down after the old woman admonished him, but I could see his fingers inching back towards the package.

Two marks under "No Kids." We were making progress.

"What about you?" the pregnant lady said to me. "You haven't said a thing so far."

"I… Well… We haven't even asked any questions yet," I said. "Feel like I wouldn't be doing my job as spokesperson if we didn't ask at least one of our three allowed questions."

"Are they capable of love?" the old woman asked, smug in what she felt would be the inevitable answer.

"How many are there?" the pregnant woman asked.

"If they kill 'em, will they like… gas 'em or…?" the young man said and then made a rudimentary gun with his fingers and made the sound of a bullet leaving the barrel with his lips.

"Again," the young woman spoke up. "Why do we care?"

"You want him to ask them why we should care?" the old man piped in. "Well, I can tell ya this much. I could care less. I want to go home."

"You mean you *couldn't* care less," the young man corrected the old man, which I could have told him was a bad idea.

"You want to hang out with these horrid mutants so bad, we'll throw you in with 'em!" the old man bared his teeth at the youth. "We'll gas and shoot the whole lot of ya!"

"The questions, people!" I got loud for the first time, because, apparently, that was the only way to be heard in this place. "We have to ask them some questions."

"We just gave you a whole passel of questions to ask," the old woman said.

"I… You… We just shouted a bunch of nonsense at each other," I replied, calming down as much as I could. "We only have three questions. We should all agree on which ones to ask before we ask them."

The old man was shaking his head. "I could care less. Or I couldn't care less. I don't give a damn! How do you like that?" he aimed his words at the young man.

Who brushed them aside. "How about this? How about we ask them if they're friendly? To, like, humans. After all, we don't want to just release them upon the world if it's gonna be a whole Planet of the Apes sort of situation. I don't think Charleton Heston here," he thumbed towards the old man, "has it left in him to put up much of a fight these days."

"You little punk. I'll show–"

"No, that's a good one," the pregnant woman stopped them. "We should ask that one. If they're friendly or if they're violent towards humans."

"Okay," I said, feeling happy again that we were finally getting somewhere, and that it was the woman next to me who was moving us along. I turned back to the TV screen, now dead and hidden in the dark. "Ma'am? Hello! We have a question!"

The screen snapped back to life. First, just a white background which forced us all to squint our eyes. Then, the smooth-featured woman with the silky voice came back into frame. "At Dotty Paradigms, we are happy to provide you with whatever information we can. This will be the first of your three questions."

184

"Are they friendly?" I asked, and then fearful of being misunderstood, "Towards humans, we mean. Are the Humanzees friendly towards humans?"

The TV woman looked off-screen for a moment as if to seek advice, nodded her chin, and turned back to us. "Only a very small sample size has had the opportunity to interact with humans, and even those have had very limited exposure. At this time, the data is inconclusive."

"Well, isn't that just great?" the young woman said.

"How about this? How much are they like us?" the young man spoke up.

"Nope!" I interrupted before the woman on the TV could respond. "We only have two questions left and any question we ask, we have to agree on beforehand. Strike that question. It doesn't count. If we have another, I'll be the one to ask it. After all, I'm the spokesperson."

"Will that be all for now?" the TV woman asked.

"Yes. Thank you," I said.

The TV winked out, and the room was, once again, a little darker.

"That would have been a good question," the boy lamented.

He was a boy too. Before, I felt he was just days into becoming a man, but I changed my mind. He was a child, in mind if not in body. And the young woman across from him so eager to kill all of these creatures, sight unseen, was equally childish, regardless of what it might say on her birth certificate.

The old woman, apparently in agreement with me, crossed her arms. "Any more brilliant interrogatives we want to waste our time with before we do the only conscionable thing there is to do and let these creatures go about their lives?"

"I'm putting my foot down on the 'no-offspring' issue," the woman next to me said and said it firmly.

185

"Can we just take a vote already so we can get out of here?" the girl said. "I mean, I think we already know how we're going to vote. Let's just be done with it."

"Alright. Okay. Fine," I said and scribbled through my previous marks so as to start fresh. "All in favor of allowing the Humanzees to live and have children?"

The old woman raised her hand as high and as proudly as she could. She was alone.

"And who's in favor of killing all of them, immediately?"

The old man and the girl raised their hands and ignored the glare from the old woman. No surprises so far.

"And who is in favor of allowing them to live, but preventing any future generations of Humanzees?"

The pregnant woman raised her hand, and slowly, less sure, so did the boy.

"Well, I suppose we can remove one of the three options," I said, getting ready to scratch through "Life" on my notepad.

"No," the old woman corrected me. "You didn't vote."

"I'm the spokesperson," I said. "I abstain."

"You can't abstain!" the girl shouted at me.

"If he can abstain, then so do I," the boy said.

"Nobody is abstaining!" the old man yelled. "Everyone votes. That's what the lying woman on the TV said, and that's what we're going to do. I voted," he jabbed a finger at his hairy chest. "They voted," he swung his long, knuckley finger at the rest of the table. "And you're going to vote too," he finished by poking me in the chest.

"Okay," I said. "Well, then in that case, I say we leave them be."

"What?" the old man erupted.

The old woman leaned back in her chair, her smile tight and content.

186

"But that's a three-way tie then," the girl said, counting out the votes on her two hands. "We have to come to a majority."

"A simple majority," the old woman said. "That means the winning side only needs three votes. Not four."

"Is that what that means?" the boy asked.

"Is that what you'd like to ask for your next question?" the angry old man said. "What's the definition of a simple majority?"

"I wanted to ask–"

"Nobody gives a damn what you wanted to ask," the old man shut him up.

"Well, somebody has to change their vote," the girl said. "Or we're never getting out of here."

"Well, I'm not changing mine," the old man said.

"And I'm not changing mine," the old woman said.

"Me neither," the pregnant woman said.

"Yep. Nope. Not me," the boy said.

"Well, then it has to be you," the girl said, staring me dead in the eyes.

"How's that supposed to work?" I said, indignant.

"Cause you were the last to vote!" the girl and the old man answered simultaneously and in stereo.

"We should ask them another question," I said. "We still have two left."

"What good is that going to do?" the girl said.

"Yeah. What are you going to ask them now?" the old man said. "If they have a soul?"

"Well, actually, that would be a really important thing to know," I said, but I don't know if I was heard. The old man's last question got the old woman fired up again, and then the room was all anger and vitriol. If there was any point in asking questions, I was beginning to doubt we'd find it. But then, the sound of tearing paper sang in the small gap between all of our words. Our eyes turned to the boy and his candy. In one hand he held an open bag of fruit snacks. In the other, he held the torn-off top of the bag.

"I got a question," he said.

The boy, of all people, surrendered his previous suggestions and, after another round of hissing and table slapping and shouting, offered a question we all deemed suitable. I managed to calm the group down and call loudly enough for the woman to return to the TV screen. When she reappeared, we all came to the subconscious group decision to present ourselves in a mannerly and courteous fashion. We all sat in our chairs, straight-backed, hands folded, eyes on the TV.

"This will be the second of your three allotted questions," the woman reminded us in her indomitably cheerful voice.

"We understand, ma'am," I told her and then asked our question. "Are they civilized?"

Again, the TV woman looked off-screen for a few seconds, nodded her head once she had the answer, and turned to face us. "The Humanzees have been provided access to education, entertainment, technologies, and comforts. They enjoy many of the advantages of what many consider to be modern, civilized life."

"Yeah, but are *they* civilized?" I repeated my question. "Not the things they have, but who they are. Are the individuals civilized? Answer the boy's question!"

"Yeah!" the boy chimed in. "Are they like us?"

"The Humanzees are very similar to you in many ways," the TV woman said without checking for an offscreen answer. "And that concludes your second and third question. Please take just a few more minutes to discuss amongst yourselves and then

188

make your decisions. Again, Dotty Paradigms thanks you for understanding the importance of your decision."

And then she was gone again.

And then there was chaos again.

"God damn you stupid good for nothing…" the old man was grabbing the boy by the clothes now and shaking him. Meanwhile, the young man only resisted by going about trying to eat his fruit snacks even as the man shook him. The old woman hopped up on her chair and screeched at the two while the girl next to her yelled "Shut up! Shut up! Shut up! Will all of you stop shouting!" while covering her ears. The pregnant woman turned away from the whole debacle and covered her eyes, saying "I can't look." The old man, apparently satisfied or perhaps just tired, shoved the boy. The boy, laughing all the while, took a whole handful of fruit snacks and slapped them into his mouth.

"That's it!" I yelled loud enough to silence all the rest. "Enough is enough! I'm changing my vote."

"You are? After that nonsense?" the old woman said.

"Yep. And because of that nonsense. After all, how can we expect them to be friendly and civilized and have a soul if they're anything like us?" I said. "Why should we plague this planet with another species that has the capability to hurt and destroy and hate but doesn't have the ability to come together to make one simple decision? If mine is the deciding vote, and it looks like it is, then I say let them die and let us all be better off for it."

"So you're going to kill them?" the old woman said.

"Listen, I didn't invent these things in a lab," I said. "This Dotty Parallelogram did. It was their idea, it's their problem, and it will be their PR nightmare if this ever gets

189

out. I say let them deal with it. And when it's all said and done, good riddance. Ma'am! Hello? Lady on the TV screen?"

With a flash of white, the monitor lit up once again. The woman on the screen with the little mouth and the pale skin and the smooth face and the big eyes came back into view. "Have you made your final decision?"

"Yes, we have," I said, speaking firmly like a spokesperson should. "The votes are in. It's one vote for letting them live as they see fit, two votes for only stopping them from having offspring, and three votes for eliminating them entirely."

"How horrible," the old woman bemoaned from across the table.

"Wild," the boy said.

"Finally," the girl said.

"We never should have been forced to make this decision to begin with," the old man said.

"We at Dotty Paradigms understand you have come to the collective decision to discontinue all living specimens of Humanzees. Our corporate leaders have elected to abide by your decision, and we will enact the elimination process as soon as possible," the woman on the TV said kindly. "Thank you again for your input on this important matter. Goodbye."

And then she was gone.

"We are getting paid, right?" the girl asked.

A door opened on the far end of the room. A different door than the one we entered, but at this point, what difference did that make? Seeing it, and understanding it meant we were to leave, the old man and the old woman both grumbled and slid down from their seats. The boy went about grabbing packages of the snacks with both hands and both feet. The girl, on the other hand, the only one of the group truly happy with the

190

results, hopped down to the floor and ran to the exit, using her knuckles to propel herself forward so she could be the first one out the door. I was second slowest to make my way toward the exit but stopped myself when I saw the pregnant woman lingering behind.

It was a significant drop from the seat to the floor, and the way she held her belly told me she was concerned about jostling her unborn child. I came to the side of her chair, placed one arm around her shoulders, and helped her down.

"Thanks," she said when we were both on the floor and making our way towards the door. "It got pretty crazy for a while there."

"Yeah. That really wasn't what I expected. Like the girl said, I thought they were going to have us pick between colors for corporate logos or say which style of car looked the fastest or… or anything but that."

"Well," she said, stopping us both before we exited the room. Beyond the doorway, the hallways were white and brightly lit. Sort of like the room the TV woman spoke to us from. "I think you did a very good job of handling the group. You were an excellent spokesperson. And I appreciate that, even though our votes were different, you were able to find a consensus."

"Yeah. Well. Compromise is important," I said, a little sheepishly.

And then she slid her foot over, laid it on top of mine, and gave my foot a gentle squeeze.

"The father? Of your baby?" I asked.

"Never knew the biological father," she said. "But I was hoping to find a good man willing to take the job."

About the Author

Joe Prosit writes sci-fi, horror, and psycho fiction. His debut novel, "Bad Brains," is followed by the "From Order Series" featuring the novels, "99 Town," "7 Androids," and "Zero City," and by his most recent novel, the psychological slasher horror "Look What You Made Me Do." He lives with his wife and kids in the Brainerd Lakes Area in northern Minnesota. If you're an adept stalker, you can find him on one of the many lakes and rivers or lost deep inside the Great North Woods. Or you can just find him on the internet at www.JoeProsit.com and follow him on X @JoeProsit for new releases and upcoming events.

Prefer to read on your device?

Go to this link and enter in the password: Ru@BadBrain? to download your free eBook version that is included in the purchase of this book.

www.ingramcontent.com/pod-product-compliance
Ingram Content Group UK Ltd.
Pitfield, Milton Keynes, MK11 3LW, UK
UKHW041317240125
4283UKWH00035B/361

9 798348 326074